5/02

The Dollmage

The Dollmage

Martine Leavitt

NORTHERN LIGHTS YOUNG NOVELS

Red Deer Press

The Publishers
Red Deer Press
813 MacKimmie Library Tower
2500 University Drive N.W.
Calgary Alberta Canada T2N 1N4
www.reddeerpress.com

Credits
Edited for the Press by Peter Carver
Cover illustration by Ron Lightburn/Limner Imagery Ltd.
Cover design by Duncan Campbell
Text design by Dennis Johnson
Printed and bound in Canada by Friesens for Red Deer Press

Acknowledgments
Financial support provided by the Canada Council, the Depart-
ment of Canadian Heritage, the Alberta Foundation for the Arts, a
beneficiary of the Lottery Fund of the Government of Alberta,
and the University of Calgary.

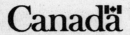

National Library of Canada Cataloguing in Publication Data

Leavitt, Martine, 1953–

The dollmage

ISBN 0-88995-233-7

1. Title

PS8573.E323D64 2001   jC813'.6   C2001-910967-9

PZ7.L4656Do 2001

5 4 3 2 1

To my parents,
James and Mary Webster,
who, in their love and wisdom,
gave me a frowning doll.

One wants a Teller in a time like this.

One's not a man, one's not a woman grown,
To bear enormous business all alone.

—"The Womanhood" from *Annie Allen*
by Gwendolyn Brooks

[Chapter 1]

MY PEOPLE, LAY DOWN YOUR STONES.

Before you stone this Annakey Rainsayer, you know it is the law and her right to have her story told. It is my duty as Dollmage to tell it. Each villager has the right to one stone, and no one will forbid you to throw it. But listen to me, and when I am done each of you will decide for yourselves if this Annakey is worthy of execution.

That is right. Lay the stones at your feet, keep them close by if it comforts you. So few of you? The stones will get heavy before the story is done.

How your hands itch to throw your stones. You hate her. You blame her for what has happened to our village. You see how I understand you? Good—now let me increase your understanding.

You see Manal standing behind me, the biggest stone of all in his hand? That stone is for whoever first casts a stone at his Annakey. He cannot fight you all, of course, but the stone he holds will take off the head of one of you. Who will be the one? Which one of you will it be?

There, I see you are now more willing to listen.

Must the ropes be so tight on her wrists? She has not tried

to escape her fate. She has broken a promise and for that she must die. This she understands.

You will not loosen them a little? Ah, Annakey, they have dragged you until your arms and back bleed and small stones are embedded in your flesh. Your face is welted and bruised. Who has been so cruel?

You, Areth? You heft your stone as one who will not rest until you have thrown it. You would willingly throw a stone at me to silence me, if you were permitted more than one, would you not? You glower at me—and so you should, for some of your story will be told tonight as well. I see it angers you, Areth, that Annakey does not weep or cower. Though she has scarcely left her girlhood, she has suffered worse hurts than these. It is Manal who weeps.

Areth, I remind you that this is the law: Before a villager can be stoned, she has the right to have her story told. Break this law and you are in danger of stoning yourself.

As for the rest of you, perhaps what makes you hasty is your fear and hunger. Greppa Lowmeadow has prepared Annakey's execution feast, a savory stew to celebrate a young woman's death. I say we eat it now, and perhaps it will quiet some of the rage in your stomachs. You will not disobey me, Greppa, though you mutter and pout. I am still your Dollmage, even now.

Listen while you eat, my people, and believe, for I am old and I have no reason any longer to lie. I no longer hear as I used to. I acquired so many brains as I aged that they press against my ears. My eyes, too, grow weaker. They have seen so much they are bored with seeing. But God sees fit not to let me lose my memory, for with it would go the memory of my sins, and God wills it that my repentance loses not its ambition. This is my repentance: to tell this story. How can I face God, my soul constipated with secrets?

The story, the story, the children say. Get on with the story. Very well, then, I will sit. Yes, yes, children, the story. Come closer, round the fire. Lay down your heavy stones. It is not your fault that you are rude and disrespectful. It is the stew's fault. How can one be patient when one's stomach is full of such gristle? Remember, Greppa, the biggest buck does not always the best stew make. What, you stiffen under the assault of my proverbs, Greppa? Think: It cannot be as bad as this stew.

I begin my story on the occasion of Annakey's birth, with the making of her promise doll. It was the day Renoa was born also, and you, Manal, and you, Areth. I grip my promise doll, symbol of the promise God has put into me. By this you know that I speak only what is true. You must forgive me as I tell the story, as I have forgiven Greppa for this stew that is like to kill me.

Now listen, and love me anyway.

[Chapter 2]

INSCRIPTION ON THE MUSIC DOLL:
Speak valley people,
make your tale heard.
You are the letters in my word.

Sing greening valleys,
rivered and long.
You are the music in my song.

THE OLDER ONES WILL REMEMBER: Annakey and Renoa were born the day my husband died.

He had been ill since the snow covered the peaks to the timberline.

"Do not die," I said to him. Was I not his Dollmage? Could I not command him?

He got worse.

"I forbid you to die," I said to him, loudly, every day.

I gave him feverfew and bloodroot and saffron tea. I made my best healing doll for him. The healing doll did not work.

With his lifeless hand in mine, I stared out my window for many hours. Four great mountains make our valley, and this day they held up the sky, a great bowl of melted blue. I could not breathe this heavy, wet sky. Outside my window I could see a bough of the plum tree. The plums baked in the sun. The bees dropped sluggishly from fruit to fruit and flew home sadly to make hot honey. My past and many years weighed down my heart, and I realized I was near the end of my powers.

I had feared for some time that my powers were getting old along with my body, and now I took my husband's death as proof. What was I to do, since I had no daughter to take my place? I was far past the age of bearing. Neither had I chosen a successor, one with the gift, to whom I could teach the art of dollmaking. Now I had expended every strength to make my man live, and I had failed. I was sure I had no power left at all. I grieved for myself and for my people.

In the evening, when my husband's body was stiff and cold, I went into my garden to comfort my heart, and found my husband's ghost hiding behind the root shed.

He beckoned to me.

"Did you not promise to die with me?" he asked. I had promised indeed, on the bed of our young love, a long time ago, as we whispered together in the dark.

Now, I loved my husband, but I did not want to go with him, not yet. I was old, but not old enough to die.

I said, "If I had found and trained my successor before this I could go with you now, husband. How many times you nagged me to do so, but I did not want to share my power. Mostly, I did not want to see that I was old." It comforted me to realize I was talking to my husband's ghost. Only one with the power of a Dollmage could see a ghost. My powers were not entirely gone yet.

"I will come back for you," he said, and he turned away.

I almost tripped over the bucket of pea pods as I ran from the root shed to the village common. Children played in the shallows where the river was widest, and farther upstream fishermen cast their lines. Youths were frog catching in the cattails, and a few girls watched them and laughed from the bucket-path. I could not die and miss these summer sights of red cows in a green field, and children splashing in the river, and the toft-gardens tumbling overgrown with vegetables. Nor could I miss the smells of sausage and cabbage and leek gravy that came out of houses as the women cooked their supper meal. I could not die and miss the merry-alder that shaded the houses, and the bright bridges that crossed the river all through the valley like stitching. How I loved the crowding forests of the uplands and the bouldered screes of the mountains. I wanted to live, and will any of you blame me?

My husband would come for me, though, as soon as my successor had been named and trained. Briefly I thought of not naming a new Dollmage, but even the thought made me tremble. What would happen to Seekvalley if I died anyway, leaving you without a Dollmage to make the story of our village? Who would make the promise dolls? It would mean the end of our people.

I stood upon Weeper's Stump and waited. I did not have long to wait. Everyone assembled quickly.

Silently, as I stood there, I prayed to God who dwells upon the mountains. I prayed to know how I should know my successor, how I should know who would have the gift to make the promise dolls.

God answered me, as he always does, but not as I had thought.

As he always does.

I saw my husband's ghost walking through the crowd, walking toward me. As he walked by Mabe Willowknot, the baby in her womb, overdue to be born by some time, leaped and kicked so that her dress jumped. It took Mabe's breath away. Ah, I thought. So that was it. My successor was not born yet.

All of you waited for my words, if not quietly, at least respectfully. I raised my hand and the crowd fell silent.

I said, "Today my successor will be born." Everyone cheered. My people, my villagers, so happy that a new Dollmage would be born that day, forgetting that it meant their old Dollmage must be losing her powers, that she may be dying. Only one person did not cheer. Only one person looked up at me sadly: Vilsa Rainsayer. She already knows, I thought. She already knows I am losing my powers. It made me angry that she knew. Vilsa always made me angry.

Perhaps that is why I chose not to see her, pregnant also, step aside to let my husband's ghost pass.

I see it now, in my mind's eye. I am forced to see, for the story is not mine, and not of my choosing. It is Annakey's story, and there is nothing like a story to make us see what we would not see. I refused to see that Vilsa had seen my husband's ghost, that perhaps, being related to me, she might have the blood of a Dollmage in her veins.

I got down from Weeper's Stump and walked back to the root shed. My husband's ghost was there, and he was shelling the peas for me.

"Husband, I cannot come with you," I said, "not now, and not next spring. The new Dollmage is not yet born."

My husband left me. I was sad because I loved him, but I was happy because now I would live.

Those of you who are old will remember how the people milled around Mabe Willowknot, congratulating her. Mabe had seven daughters. I knew when she had this eighth daughter she would be happy enough to let me have her and raise her.

There had been one cloud on Mount Crownantler that morning. By midday the whole west sky was black with clouds, and at evening meal the storm broke.

"Mabe Willowknot labors with child," Gilly Post reported

to me, her face lit by distant lightning. I nodded and sent her away. I was making a trail of peas from the root shed to the bedroom in the hopes that I could entice my husband's spirit to sleep with me that night. Now that I knew I would live, I missed him.

Someone else came to the door. The child is born already, I thought.

"Dollmage, I have news." It was Greppa Lowmeadow's oldest child, dripping with rain at my door.

"Well?"

"My mother has gone early into childbirth."

I did not answer. Once again, God had tricked me. We are friends that way.

"And Norda Bantercross, also, Dollmage. And Vilsa Rainsayer."

Greppa's child shrank back a little at the sight of my face, and then ran away when I began to laugh. When my laughter was spent, I wept. It was the first time I had wept since my husband died. I wept to lose him, the one who had been my husband, my child, my friend—and then I wept to lose my powers. Here was more proof that I was dwindling in power, for I had not foreseen that more than one child would be born. I prayed for three boys and only one girl. I prayed to have power enough to be Dollmage for my people until the next Dollmage was old enough. When I had done with tears, I picked up the peas one by one and ate them and mourned out my mourning.

That night, in the lightning and thunder, four children were born into the village. To Norda Bantercross was born a son, who she named Manal after her dead husband; to Greppa Lowmeadow a son, who she called Areth because she had no taste; and to Mabe Willowknot, a daughter she named

Renoa. But God loved me so much he chose not to make my life too easy. Vilsa also was delivered of a daughter, who she named Annakey.

Now this was a puzzle indeed. "Which girl is the Dollmage?" the villagers asked. You older ones will remember how you asked me in just this way: "Which baby girl is the Dollmage? Which girl will have the gift and power to make promise dolls for our people, to make the story of our village?"

I stared at you. I did not know how to answer.

Finally I said, "The promise dolls will tell."

But I had already decided in my heart that it must be Mabe Willownot's daughter, Renoa. Why? I will tell you the truth. I had more than one reason to dislike Vilsa Rainsayer.

THIS IS WHY I did not like Vilsa Rainsayer, even though she was my distant cousin. First, her house was always cleaner than mine. A woman who keeps her house so clean is asking to be disliked. Once I had tried sprinkling a little dust over her house in the village doll. It hadn't worked at all. The next day I went to her house and it was cleaner than ever. My husband said, "Perhaps she has a little power of her own. Is she not your relative? Perhaps it is only enough to resist the story you make of her in the village doll." His suggestion infuriated me, but not as much as what he said next.

He said she was beautiful. That is the second reason I disliked her. Since I loved my husband, there was no one to blame but her.

Do you think I enjoy confessing all my niggling faults? But if I must do it, be sure I will tell yours, also. How many of you harbor little resentments, almost invisible envyings? How many of you, when you hear of another's misfortune, before you have had time to train your heart to be sad, feel first a tiny thrill of gladness? Ah, you think in the secret corners of your brains, because it has happened to him, it has not happened to me. If only for today, life has been kinder to me, and though I am not so fair or rich or strong or wise as he, I am unafflicted by his sorrow. Now you will see what great sadnesses can come from such tiny prides and baby hates.

Now I will tell you the third and biggest reason why I disliked Vilsa.

The fall before Annakey and Renoa and Manal and Areth were born, Vilsa's husband, with another man, went away to look for another valley. "There will not be enough land for our son's sons," Fedr Rainsayer had declared at a village meeting.

You older ones will remember. Fedr said, "My tally stick says in the next generation there will be dearth."

"There are no more valleys," I told him at the meeting. "The valley where my great-grandmother lived was taken over and infested by robber people. All the villages around were destroyed. Only we survived. We came here to the only other valley that could be found in the endless range of mountains that make up our world."

"We have no choice but to look," Fedr said gravely. "We must think of our children and our grandchildren."

I shrugged my shoulders. "You are going to your deaths," I said.

Then Vilsa Rainsayer spoke up. "Dollmage, where is your faith? Is this not your art? Do you not remember that when our great-grandmother was young and the robber people came, she made a doll of this valley? She made it first, and so it was found, and so we live here. Could you not make a doll of another valley?"

"Of course I remember," I said. "I care for the village doll she made to this day. I add to it. Nothing is built in the village until it is first added to the valley doll. I make the story of the village by it." But my pride was damaged. How dare she instruct me, I thought.

Vilsa's voice became gentle, and she touched my hand. "Make us a doll of a new valley, and my husband will find it. Make him safe among the deep passes and the slag peaks, Dollmage, and he will find a new valley."

Now I knew her gentleness was to appease me, but it offended me almost worse than her instructions. I tried to make a new valley doll but my pride was taking up all the room in my heart. There was no room left for my art to breathe. Also, I was not so young as my great-grandmother had been when she made a new valley doll.

I tried to make something. I tried, but it would not come. I might have seen even then that my powers were dwindling, but at the time I blamed Vilsa. I thought, I cannot make the doll of a village that is not there. Well, she would have something, and so I got out my materials and began. Finally I fashioned something, a valley held by five mountains. It was done. There were crags and water and wild forests. There were pines on the stony slopes, and flowering oak and blue-holly on the valley floor. To the untrained eye it was sufficient, but I knew that it had not come from any place real.

When I showed it to the men who journeyed, they looked at it solemnly and nodded and said good-bye. Vilsa Rainsayer, when she looked at it, however, was not pleased.

"Dollmage, is there no deer-trod in the thicket?" she asked.

"There is game. It is midday and the hart sleeps."

"Dollmage, where are the roosting birds and the mice and the owls?" she asked.

19

"Sleeping in their holes," I said sharply.

She looked puzzled. "I see no dens, no nests." She walked around it. "Is there no cornflower in the meadow? Is there no nettle? No wild corn or creepers?"

I glared at her. I hated her then. How dare she criticize! She as much as said she saw no art in it, no dreaming, no vision, and she might have found no better way to insult me.

She became afraid for her husband and begged him not to leave. He and his companion, Petr, the fieldmaster's hermit brother, disappeared into the mountain forest. When they were gone, I took the new valley doll.

I meant to set it on the floor in the corner, but it slipped out of my hands.

It smashed against the wall, breaking, and the small pieces I had made for men flew onto the dirt floor. It was dark. I looked for them on my hands and knees, sick in my heart. I could not find them. After a time I gave up, and left the mess in a dark corner of the room for the mice to gnaw and the beetles to crawl upon.

"Well," I said to the dark in the room, "I told them they were going to their deaths."

The guiltier I felt, the more I blamed Vilsa. When it was known in the village that Vilsa had a child growing in her, I began to despise her. God had not sent me a child. To make things worse, though she was pregnant, she was still beautiful, and her house was still cleaner than mine.

Now you know why I did not like Vilsa Rainsayer. When she gave birth to a daughter on the same day as Mabe Willowknot, I liked her even less. I asked God why he was doing this to me. "To make you wise," he said. I was surprised. I was already very wise.

THE THUNDERSTORMS CEASED in the night and the dawn rose on sleet showers. I went to visit Mabe Willowknot. The turf in the village common was spongy underfoot so I did not frighten the swans that fed on the river, nor did Mabe hear me coming. Her infant child was crying, but Mabe lay unconcerned.

"Let her sisters pick her up," she said to my cross look. "I've fed the child." She was a winter peach: sour, and at her center a hard core.

"What will you name her?"

She shrugged. I named the child Renoa after the baby I never had, and I began to love her.

Then I went to see Vilsa Rainsayer. Her roof needed thatch, and the shed door was in poor repair, but what was to be expected? Her husband had still not returned. When people suggested that she mourn for her husband, she only laughed. She refused to believe that he was dead. She was a quiet lass, but bone stubborn.

Vilsa sat in a rocker, cradling her babe as if she had given birth to her own heart. The floor of stone flags was clean as a river pebble. Before the fire were two sturdy chairs, and on them were thick, soft cushions, newly sewn, the stuffing smelling sweet of ladies' bedstraw. The fire was cheery, the mantel dusted, the hearthstone scrubbed, and the chimney breast decorated with a swag of dried flowers. The pottery sink was without stain, the cream pans were polished, and the kettle scrubbed. Through the bedroom door I could see a bed, thick with quilted comforters, and a few worn clothes hung clean and mended on hooks. A chest at the foot of the bed had been freshly oiled. There were clover tarts in a basket on the table, the scent of them warming the house as much as the fire. I love clover tarts, but today the smell of them made me gag.

"How could you clean today?" I asked.

She was pale, but prettier for it. "My friends have been kind," Vilsa said.

"You were not supposed to be the one," I said to her.

"Forgive me, Dollmage, but is God not the one who gave me to deliver in the storm?" Her voice was deferent, but strong in the truth. When was she going to learn not to be more right than me?

"Perhaps," I said, "but she will not be Dollmage."

"Have you made her promise doll already?" she asked, surprised.

"No."

"Then we will see."

She did not see that I wanted to slap her for her insolence. Everyone else feared and flattered me, and I had become used to it.

She could not keep her eyes off her baby child. Why did that also cause me a small pain at the back of my heart?

"What will you name her?" I asked in the most civil tone I could manage.

"Annakey, for her father loves that name."

"Let me give you some advice," I said.

"Yes, Dollmage."

"It is foolish to love your Annakey so. A child who is adored and meets with nothing but kindness in its own home will be baffled when it meets the world full of greed and cruelty. A child who is protected does not learn to fight, does not learn to be wary and sly."

Vilsa smiled and said respectfully, "Dollmage, did our grandmother not teach us that a child who is loved in her own home will grow to look for love everywhere?"

Why must she remind me of our shared heritage? Why must she ever contradict me?

She saw my look and said quietly, "Dollmage, in my joy for my child, I have forgotten your sorrow in losing your husband. I am so sorry for your loss."

"Your husband, too, is dead," I said. I wanted to hurt her. Had she not hurt me?

She looked at me for a long moment. She was pale from childbirth, but she became even paler then. Finally, she shook her head. "I would know."

"You cannot know."

"Dollmage, you have made a valley doll. My husband had great faith in your art. He will find the valley, and then he will return."

"If he does not, it will not be my fault," I said. "I told you all before I made it that there is nothing beyond these mountains."

Vilsa looked down at her child and held her even more tightly. "My husband will come home with a story to tell."

Then she forgot me, and began to sing to her child a sweet song of love. Vilsa's husband was gone, but God had given her a child to comfort her heart.

SUMMER TURNED INTO FALL as I found the perfect wood for each infant's doll. I fasted and prayed to find the promise that lay hidden within.

It did not come to me. It would not. I went without sleep many nights. One day I went to Mabe Willowknot's home. I picked up the baby Renoa and took her to my house.

"Poor babe," I said. "You waited too long to come, and now there is no power in me even to make you a promise doll."

Baby Renoa began to wail, but even as she did, I knew how to make Manal's promise doll. I let God guide my hands as I carved away the wood that hid the promise of the child's life. When it was done, I knew how to make Areth's, and then the dolls of the infant girls. I borrowed on tiny Renoa's powers.

One day I climbed upon Weeper's Stump to announce the day of the promise doll ceremony for the four babies. As you gathered, I rejoiced to be alive, and to have found a way to serve you until Renoa was old enough. I rejoiced in our good valley, for black cows in a gold field, and for white geese growing fat on the hay stubble. My husband's ghost was nowhere to be seen.

"The promise doll ceremony for Renoa, Annakey, Manal, and Areth will be at the next full moon," I said.

Many tried to find out about the dolls before the ceremony. Some asked subtle questions and reminded me of all the favors they had done for me. Some brought whitemeats and puddings to my door and tried peeking around while I thanked them. It was for naught. I had hidden the dolls in the secret, locked room of my house.

BEFORE SUNRISE, on the day of the promise doll ceremony for the new babies, the women were moving quietly in the dark, covering the tables in the village common with hot bread, with dishes of fresh butter, stewed fruits, crisped saltmeats, baked brown eggs, and baskets of sweet buns. Milk still warm from the cows' udders steamed from clay jugs.

The sun rose while the moon was still in the sky. Men and children tumbled out of their cottages and crossed the arched bridges to the common. The mountain forests gleamed green, polished by the heavy rains. The mountaintops were blue and there was no snow on them. The rushy waters of Shrink Creek were swollen to the tops of the banks, spilling over in places throughout the valley to water the fields already deep in corn. It was an auspicious day.

As the villagers gathered, they eyed the food but they would not touch it until after the ceremony. The four new mothers, holding their infants, stood in the center of the common. One by one I would hang the promise dolls, each as small as a child's thumb, round the necks of the infants in the presence of the witnesses.

Because it was the day I would give the promise doll to the new Dollmage, I had also made memory dolls for each member of the village.

"Take them," I said as you assembled. "Take them, one to a person. There are some of cloth and some of wax. Here, for you, the one who lingers in the back, who did not reach out to grab—for you, I have a glass one. Put it in the window of your home and see what happens. Here, little ones, whose arms are short for the grabbing, I have dolls filled with pebbles and corn and wheat, and for the infants I have some filled with horsehair or sheep's wool or feathers."

You pressed around me, my people, talking and laughing, for your memory dolls. Some of you did not want memory dolls, for you saw no benefit in remembering. To those I gave dolls with more than one purpose. For those, I had dolls with beaks and bills and snouts. "As you keep them," I said, "so will your barnyard animals be healthy and avoid hoofrot and lice." I may have forgotten to tell them that their memories, too, would have beaks and bills. That is what you get.

For a woman whose child whimpered at her breast, I had a fever doll, and for Old Man Peel, who had many sins, I gave a memory doll that was also a mercy doll. "Who said old age is a time of rest?" I said as I gave it to him.

Finally, when everyone had been given his gift, I stood

upon Weeper's Stump. In the ritual way I said, "God has given me the gift to fashion the god of your spirit. It is my gift and power to do so, and will any of you gainsay it?" Normally I do not wait for an answer, but today I let the silence hang in the air for a time.

"So have I done for the four babes." I cleared my throat. "I have used two different types of wood for the boys, but the same wise beech for the girls. With my knife and many incantations I have carved the woods into small totems, each with ear markings, to ensure that we hear the promises others make and so encourage them in the keeping of those promises. Each has eye markings, so they can watch that we keep the promises we ourselves make. The other markings are different for each child. The markings of a Dollmage are given to none else. The powers of a Dollmage are breathed upon her by God, fallen down from heaven, dream-given. It is the gift. It cannot be taught or learned. It comes out of the sky and lands in a baby when she is born. The only things that can be learned are the dollmaking skills, and the ability to interpret the promise God has given each soul." The crowd looked up at me expectantly, but some murmured among themselves.

"What is it?" I asked. No one answered.

"What is it?" I asked again.

Only Oda Weedbridge had the courage to speak up. "Dollmage," she said, "they are wondering how you made promise dolls for the two girls, both born on the day upon which the Dollmage was to be born."

I smiled patiently and nodded. "I will reveal to you now what I did. Both girls' promise dolls have the eyes of a Dollmage: slightly askant so they may not see the world straight on, but that they might see under the corners of the everyday world. As I made them I will confess to you that I was amazed. How, I asked God, can there be two? I had searched the scripts of the Sacred dolls, and the law was clear: There shall be only one Dollmage in one village.

"Then God told me what to do, something that I have never seen done before. I made an important difference in the promise dolls. Then, he told me to allow the babes to choose before all the people."

There was a silence, then a murmuring of agreement, and I could see that you, my people, loved me for my wisdom. Is it my fault? I told you clear as clear that God had given me the wisdom. If you still chose to honor me instead, it could hardly be my fault.

"These children," I said, "are like the mountains that cradle our valley. Out of storm were they born, but they will be unmoved. They will have stories told of them. For Greppa Lowmeadow's son, Areth, I have made a beautiful promise doll. Like Southslope Mountain, he will be fair of face. Remember, though, that Southslope Mountain in winter can send down the avalanche. Areth must make sure winter never lives in his heart."

I hung the doll around the infant's neck and everyone clapped.

"For Norda Bantercross's son, Manal, I have made a doll from most precious wood. He will be strong, like Mount Crownantler, tall and full of weather. His soul will run with the wild game, he will drink from cold rivers and be free. A compass is carved upon the doll, for all things will be measured by him."

I hung the doll around the infant's neck and everyone clapped. Norda held her child up high for all to see. There was gentle laughter.

I gestured and Mabe Willowknot and Vilsa Rainsayer came forward with their babies. Vilsa's face was radiant with joy. In her eyes was so much trust and humility before my power that for a moment my heart smote me. I remembered then that she had been an obedient and respectful girl all her life. I remembered that she had come to my bed of mourning to oil and rub my feet, and that her tears had fallen on my ankles. Her own husband was gone, and though she refused to believe that he was dead, she knew how gray was my world. I remembered that she always agreed with me at meeting in the House of Women. Though the babies would choose the promise doll they wanted, I knew which one would get which. Knowing what would be leftover for Vilsa's child Annakey, I had felt a secret gladness. Now, I felt sorry. I realized what a cruel thing it was, and I was sorry.

Even the children in the crowd were silent now. I held up the promise dolls for all to see, just within reach of the babes' little hands and bright eyes. There was a gasp, as I thought there would be.

One of the promise dolls had a smile and hung true. The other promise doll hung crookedy, and on its small face was a frown.

Both mothers hesitated when they saw the frowning promise doll. Even Mabe, who hardly heard her child's cries in her indifference, seemed unwilling to give her baby the fate such a promise doll would suggest.

I dangled the dolls before the babies. They smiled, cooed, and both reached out for the promise dolls. Both reached out for the frowning promise doll.

I was aghast. Both baby girls had grasped the frowning promise doll and were tugging at it. Renoa, being the lustier, snatched it away from Annakey and put the cord in her mouth. Annakey began to wail.

"She wants it," the people around her said.

"Give her the other promise doll to comfort her."

Unwillingly, I placed the smiling promise doll in Annakey's hand. She threw it away and wailed even more loudly.

The crowd became noisy. Vilsa was silent and pale. I picked up the smiling promise doll and put it in Renoa's hand. Greedily she grabbed onto it, and dropped the frowning doll. I put the frowning doll in Annakey's hand, and instantly she was silent.

The outcry died down at the same time that Annakey's cries were stilled.

"Well," I said. I did not look at Vilsa. God had decided. I placed the soggy, smiling promise doll around Renoa's neck. "Renoa has a promise doll with the eyes of a Dollmage. She will see behind things and under things. Like Mount Lair, she will be wild and beautiful. Though Mount Lair is pathless, she will make paths."

Everyone clapped and cheered. They gathered around Mabe and her child, almost forgetting that there was another child to be done. Small children began stealing eggs from the table. I held up my hand and the crowd settled a little. I placed the frowning promise doll around Annakey's neck.

"This child's doll, too, has the eyes of a Dollmage—slightly askant, so that she might see netherworlds and things meant to be. But this child will be like the valley that is not yet found."

Vilsa looked at me with great eyes, her face open and vulnerable, willing still to trust me. But in my face she saw that I thought it was a bad omen, and she dropped her eyes. I saw her look into the sweet sleeping face of her baby.

No one clapped. A few murmured. There was a wind in the beeches, and a single black swan rose from the river thicket.

"What does the frown mean, Dollmage?" Vilsa asked low.

Now, I had obeyed God, but the truth was I did not know the meaning of the frown. Unwilling to appear ignorant before my people, I said, "She will be sad because she cannot be Dollmage."

Vilsa was silent and still. Everyone stared at her, sorry for her but glad it had not happened to them. There were a few murmurs of sympathy, and a few people whispering all the reasons they thought Vilsa may have deserved what had happened. It is important to make people deserve what happens to them. If bad things can happen for no apparent reason, then bad things might happen to innocent us.

Vilsa then turned toward her fellow villagers, head held high, and did an unthinkable thing. Grasping her promise doll, she made a promise.

"I promise," she said clearly, "that my child will be happy." The crowd fell utterly silent.

I was not sorry anymore. How dare she challenge my art! If I put a frown on her daughter's doll, then frown she would.

"Fool!" I said to Vilsa before the whole village. "You make a promise for another's life, and so it must come out of your own doll. If your daughter is happy, it will be because you are not."

Vilsa bent her head and walked away.

My mother once told me that every tear I cause another to cry would be gathered by God, that one day he would boil the tears to their hottest point and drip them upon me one by one. When I was very young, I was cautious. As a youth, however, I knew that what she said was a lie, and I caused many tears to fall. In my old age, I know it is true. The single tear Vilsa shed as she walked proudly back to her house drips hot down my heart even now.

[Chapter 3]

INSCRIPTION ON THE LORE DOLL:
The mother of our people was not in
the mountains two months, but ten.
And not with maids only, but men.

NOW, WE ARE A PEOPLE born into many promises. We promise to keep our promises, and we promise not to lie. That is enough for one life. But there are other promises. We promise to be the best friend of one other person in the world, and to be on his or her side whenever there is a side to be on. That is why, my people, if you will not free Annakey's hands, I command you as Doll-mage to let Manal give water to his Annakey, his best friend. Put down your rock, Manal. No one will hurt her until I have done speaking. It is the law. No? You will not? To look at Areth, I see that once again you are wise. Furthermore, the villagers do not soften their gaze, even to remember Annakey as an infant. How can they forget their hate when all around them is the consequence of her broken promise? Since the beginning we have been warned: One broken promise can a people break. Now we see it is true. Though I tell the story with great wit and talent, it may be required of you both to die this day.

But you, Dantu, and you, Tawm, I see you have thrown your rocks away. Do you have the courage to loosen the ropes at Annakey's wrists? There. There. A little longer and she would have lost her hands. Why this comforts me, I do not know. What matters hands if she is dead?

Now, where was I? Oh, yes, our other promises. We promise to feed our child and care for it until it becomes independent enough to be ungrateful. We promise to be inoffensive to others, which means we keep our bodies washed, our yards kept, our children quiet, and our outhouses downhill. These alone are enough promises to fill a whole day, every day. But there is more. We promise to bring peace and safety to our people by living wisely, working hard, and helping our neighbors. We promise to care for our old folk and to be faithful to our mates.

Our promises are what separate us from the robber people that infest the mountains around us. They beat and abuse their children, abandon the weak and old, leave their mates for any other that may come along, and love to live off the labor of others. Without the promise, we would be nothing more than they. It is what keeps us strong as a people. To break a promise is to bring weakness, sadness, even destruction to our people.

So you see why to grasp one's promise doll and make a promise before a congregation is a rash thing. To make a promise such as the one Vilsa made then was a danger.

IT WENT ACCORDING TO MY WORD. As if there were only so much happiness to be found in the world, all the happiness drained out of Vilsa's life after that day so that it might be given to her daughter. She was more silent than before, more watchful for her husband who every day did not return. Year after year she did her work soberly so that I could not find fault. She also did the work of others in exchange for repairs to be done on her house. Year after year, she would stop in the middle of feeding the chickens or slopping the hog or weeding the garden, and she would stand and look past the grain fields to the deep and sunless woodland, and past the woodland to the uplands where only furze and bramble grew, until finally her eye would search the snowline. Never did she see a man come. Her eyes would go back to her work, dull with always searching and never seeing.

Only when she looked at her daughter, Annakey, did her face shine with joy. Only at the sound of her daughter's laughter would she smile.

Annakey grew tall, dark-haired like her father and pretty like her mother, and as she grew, so too did my resentment. I had carved a frown into her promise doll, but the child never ceased to smile and laugh and sing. Even when her face was in repose, her lips curled up at the corners so that she appeared to be on the verge of smiling.

Only now, when her lips are swollen and bloodied, can I see no trace of a smile. This brings me no happiness, but at the time I was angered that Vilsa's promise could be so powerful. It humiliated me to look at the child. I had made a frown on her promise doll. When would she frown? I began to think that she smiled just to show everyone in the village that my powers were aging.

I took revenge in subtle ways, in ways so soft and sly that I was able to keep them secret even from myself. I do not wish to tell you this, but I am compelled, for I am no longer in control of the story. Though it was often my lot to help villagers in need, I was usually silent on the subject of Vilsa. If someone came to me with extra wheat, or whitemeats, or a bushel of fruit, I would give it to someone else in need before I gave it to Vilsa. Vilsa only worked harder, and grew thinner and paler and more beautiful. I gave Vilsa the worst of the cast-off clothing that was mine to distribute, but she mended and altered and embroidered the things I gave her so that Annakey might be as charmingly dressed as any. Worst of all, year after year she kept her house cleaner than mine. She was a cliff-lily: delicate but tenacious, able to cling to the barest rock wall.

As Annakey grew I feared what she might do, having the promise doll of a Dollmage, but not her gift. Would she have a kind of power? Would she abuse it? I watched her hard as a toddler and as a young child, and I was strict with her. I saw no great fault in her, but just to be sure, when she seemed loud or overactive or selfish, I corrected her.

Still, she was always cheerful. One year, at the celebration of the Planter's Moon, when all the children get large brittle-candy moons and suck on them slowly, Renoa bumped Annakey. Her moon fell to the floor and broke into pieces. Everyone around her made small sounds of sympathy, waiting for tears. Any child would have cried a little. Annakey knelt down, picked up the pieces, said, "Look, now I have a lot of little moons. Here is a crescent moon, and this one is jagged like a star. . . ."

She frightened me.

Now, Renoa grew up the youngest of eight sisters. She was neglected by her mother and bullied by her sisters. Though her promise doll smiled, Renoa's face was brown as bark, and stern. I pitied her and tried to protect her from her mother and her overbearing sisters. I babysat her when her mother was sick, which was often, and let her come into my house. Everyone looked on in envy for this rare privilege. I told her that her life would be better than that of her sisters. Not for her a life of cooking and weeding and scrubbing and chores. Others would do much of this for her while she practiced her art. I talked to her about the Sacred dolls, and told her stories, but she yawned and gazed longingly out the window.

Of course it was a mistake. I meant to encourage her. Instead she began to despise the people she must serve. Her sisters' meanness did not make her meek and sensitive, it only made her mean. She ran away from them and me, and hid in the forests and glades of Mount Lair. She knew no one could find her there where there were no paths. She came to know where the berry bushes were, and the streams, and the beneficent roots and mushrooms. As she grew older, excused from women's work because of her calling, she stayed away for whole days at a time. Nevertheless, she began to show at an early age that she had a gift.

How could she not be imbued with the spirit of my gift, surrounded as she was with the makings of my magic? She had free access to my shelves and tables, covered with cloth and wood bits, with thread and odds of fur and ribbons and buttons. Every barrel, kettle, and crock was heaped with the stuff of my craft, and it was hers to explore. I gave her my baskets to dip into, full of bones and barley, teeth and shells, seeds, antlers, and colored glass. I let her play with any doll she might see: dolls made of clay and cookie, wire and wadding, apples, potatoes, socks, and bottles. When she was only five years old, I made her help in the making of Elna Greenpea's worry doll. Remember, Elna, that you worried your daughter would marry someone with a temperament like your husband's? After you received the worry doll, your daughter married instead a man with a temperament like yours. Your worries were over as your troubles began.

One day, when Renoa was still young, I forced her to make a one-handed beggar doll for Kopper Looseniggle. Kopper had borrowed a hammer from his neighbor and now claimed he had lost it. Now, here is a problem. Had Kopper truly lost the hammer? Or was he breaking his promise not to steal? If Kopper was innocent, the doll would help him find the hammer. If he was guilty, he would become just like the doll with only one hand. He would never know when it would happen, but someday, somehow, Kopper would lose his hand. Renoa was intrigued by the thought of making the doll, but refused to do so until I agreed to leave her alone to do it. I left and she made a fine doll indeed.

Renoa gave Kopper the doll and then followed him around for days, waiting and watching. The doll worked. He found the hammer.

Renoa was disappointed, bored, and lost interest in doll-making just when I was about to name her as the new Doll-mage. "When I am older, Dollmage," she said as she ran away to play in the forests of the mountains like a wild thing.

I let her go, for I had seen my husband's ghost lurking at the outskirts of the village. When he came to me that evening, I said, "Another year, and then she will be ready."

After that I went home and made a ghost doll. I named it after my husband and put it deep into the forest where it would be hard for him to find his way out again. I loved my husband, but I was not ready to die.

Renoa grew strong and fearless. The people liked her, not only because one day she would be their Dollmage, but also because of her easy way with them. They thought she was familiar with them because she liked them. In truth, she was at her ease because she cared not a whit for their opinion. She had a way with animals as well. The orneriest cow would give milk for her. The dogs of the village became still for her, followed her about when she let them, as if she were their owner. Always she smelled of green herbs, sweet-scented. Often she did not return home from the mountain wood until late, ravenous and moon-glad. I loved her as the child I did not have, and so I was patient. I would let her have her childhood as I did not have mine.

From my earliest memories my grandmother made me study and practice the art of dollmaking, until my soft little fingers bled and became calloused. While other children played, I studied and worked, collected materials and sorted them. I made doll after doll, only to have my grandmother throw them away and instruct me to begin again.

My grandmother taught me that a Dollmage must have both gift and skill. The gift I had, but the skill came only with tears and much rapping of knuckles. Renoa, it seemed, would be like me. I would give her another year. Or two.

It had become easy for me to continue as Dollmage as soon as Renoa was born. I was able to borrow upon her powers, and I supposed I would until the day came when she was formally named Dollmage.

ANNAKEY, AS SOON AS SHE WAS ABLE, was required to go into the fields to watch the sheep. In this way she earned mutton and wool for her mother. Though she could not spend her days playing with the other girls, still Annakey smiled.

Mostly I forgot about her, until one day I saw her by the river collecting stones that looked like animals or faces of people she knew.

"Have you not enough work to do?" I asked her. She dropped the stones into the water and ran away. How well I remembered my own passion for the miniature, the copy, and it concerned me to see what might be the beginnings of it in Annakey.

I asked Grandmother Keepmoney to observe her, to see if she worked worthy of the hire.

"She does," said Grandmother Keepmoney.

"Then why does she smile so, seeing she must work?" I asked my friend.

"Herding sheep is light enough work. She plays with the boys, with Areth and Manal and the others. They are happy in the fields because there are no adults to restrict them."

"And what do they play at?" I asked.

"They play at being adults. They pretend marrying and babies and cooking and milking cows. They pretend storms and bears and raids from robber people. The boys love Annakey."

"So," I said. "They run away from their parents' world only to build a make-believe world just like it."

"Has it not always been so, Hobblefoot?" Grandmother Keepmoney said. "When you and I were young, did you not make cookies and babydolls of clay? Even in your play you were Dollmage."

What she said was true. Thinking about what she had said made me uneasy about Annakey. What if she was growing Dollmage powers right under my chin? I decided to spy on her.

Annakey was a monster in my eyes—given the eyes of a Dollmage only because she was born on the promised day. She must never be allowed to practice any art she might have. It would cause confusion, disharmony, turmoil. It would split the valley, and the wild all around would creep in. She was a weed allowed to thrive in a garden.

I found the children in a little grove of trees in the west field. Most of the sheep were tended in the summer meadow high on the mountain, but some, lambs born too early or rams and ewes that were too old, stayed in the valley. Young children, field size, kept them. It was lazy work. They had only to keep the stock away from the drifts of bracken that marked the edge of the forest. Bears and wolves rarely came here, but there were foxes, and bogs to fall into.

As it was, only Manal was at his post with the sheep. The others were in a small grove of trees, seated around a tree stump that served as a table. There were seven boys: Areth Lowmeadow, Miller Gravepost, Nikko Nailsmith, Surry Wistnot, Dantu Three, Nid Maybenot, and Tawm Herdson. One girl: Annakey Rainsayer. They were all looking at her with adoration. Oblivious to their love, she was serving them, solemnly and with tender pats to their heads, wild berries in dried mud bowls.

The bowls were small, but perfectly made. In the center of the stump was a graceful clay vase and in that, a flower. In Annakey's arms was a baby made of bark and branches and grass and leaves, all tied and knotted in clever ways so that it was easy to see it was a baby. She cradled the baby in one arm and poured water from a little clay pitcher into little clay cups for the boys.

"Am I not the best of all your children?" Surry asked quietly as Annakey poured him water.

"If she says yes, I shall black your eye later," said Nid mildly and with a ferocious smile.

"I am the one who gathered the berries. She loves me best," said Miller in his sweetest voice, as if he had just given the boys a generous compliment.

"Dullwits," said Dantu gently and graciously. "It is easy to see why you love me best, Annakey, since they are all so lump-brained."

Annakey stopped pouring water. "Did I not speak to all of you about quarreling?" she said.

"You told us to speak in kindly tones," Areth said, grinning. "Their tones sound kindly to me."

The boys laughed, and then the laughter faded under Annakey's stern gaze.

"All of you go play," said Areth to the others. He was a head taller than the rest of them.

"I do not want to go," said Dantu.

"Yes, we do not want to go, too."

"You must go. Gather deadfall for the supper fire," Areth said.

"Why must we always go?" Tawm protested.

"Because," said Areth, "you are the children and I am the father. Now go. I want to speak to your mother alone for a moment."

One by one, the other boys tumbled out of the grove and ran to the field where the sheep slept like lumps of wool in the deep grass. As soon as they were alone, Areth took Annakey's hand.

"Annakey," he said, "promise me you will be my wife."

"I am already your wife," Annakey said.

"I mean for real. When we grow up."

Annakey drew her hand away and laughed. "Areth, what if I grow up to be nagging and ugly?" The child seemed a little afraid, as if she understood at a level beyond her years the nature of such a promise.

Just then Manal entered the grove.

Annakey held up a bowl of berries for him. "Areth wants me to promise to be his wife," she said.

Manal said nothing. His manner was gentle and quiet. Areth lay down in the grass to sulk. Annakey watched as Manal ate the berries, looking into his bowl.

They talked quietly. Manal told Annakey how Papa Naplong's hog, wandering the fringes of the forest for worms and mice, had come upon a newborn lamb to eat it. Manal had had to chase him away with a stick.

"That is good, Manal," Annakey said.

Manal shrugged. "It is my work, to care for the sheep."

"Manal, why do you work with the sheep while the rest of us play?" she asked.

"You play at women's work," Manal said.

"It makes me happy to do so," Annakey said, after a moment's thought.

Manal glanced at her and almost smiled. "Work makes me . . . happy." He ate in silence for a time and then said, "These bowls are good, Annakey. They make the food taste better."

I almost gasped aloud.

Annakey picked one up and inspected it closely to hide her blushes. She shook her head.

"And the babydoll is as good as one of Dollmage's."

That part was not true.

"If I were Dollmage," Annakey said, "I would use my power to make my father come home."

Manal stood. "By now the others are fighting amongst themselves and have forgotten the sheep." He began to walk away but stopped before Areth. "Dollmage teaches that we are born into enough promises," he said to him. Then he was gone.

I could hardly hear what was being said because my eyes were studying the bowls, the vase, and the babydoll too hard. Finally I decided the bowls were just homely toys, and nothing to punish her about. Still, it must be stopped. I emerged from my hiding place, startling Annakey and Areth.

"Hello, Grandmother Dollmage."

Closer up, I could see that the bowls were clever indeed. For a moment the valley rocked beneath my feet. Then I saw the stubble geese squawking in the mown fields, and the hogs grunting after the acorn harvest at the wood's edge, and the boys bleating among the sheep. All was as it should be, I told myself.

"You are too old to be with the boys now," I said. "Go home, and tell your mother that she should be teaching you the arts of sewing and cooking and gardening."

"Can we play later?" Areth said to her as she stood, cradling her babydoll.

"She will be too busy to play, for a long time," I said.

She began to walk away with the babydoll. I thought to see a frown on her face, but she did not frown. "Perhaps, like Manal, I will find work better than play," she said.

"Leave the baby, child," I said.

She turned and looked at me for a long moment, and then put the babydoll carefully on the stump. She smoothed her skirt.

"Leave her," I said, "and make no more dolls. You are forbidden."

She stood still, looking at her babydoll, her hands at her sides trembling. "Her name is Nesbeth," she said quietly and clearly.

Slowly she began to walk away again. Once, she stopped and looked back at the baby, and then she ran.

Areth kicked the ground sullenly and went to check on the sheep. When he was out of sight, I smashed the clever bowls and the vase. I took the babydoll home to give to my pig to eat.

FOR RENOA'S ELEVENTH BIRTHDAY I determined that I would make her a gift. I made a play doll of the finest clay, fired and painted and polished it until it was an exact replica of Renoa herself. I dressed it in fine lavender wool and plaited cornsilk for its hair. Even Renoa's mother, when I presented it to her, was enchanted. Renoa tugged on the child doll's hair, lifted her skirt, and scratched at its painted lips. Then she laid down the doll and ran off to play in the forest.

"She wastes her talent," I said to her mother.

"It is not my fault," Mabe said sullenly. "You chose her."

"God chose her."

"Then it is God's Fault. Capital *F*. Maybe it is to be Annakey after all."

"No," I said. "Annakey's promise doll has a frown. The bore hole in her doll is crookedy."

"The villagers say until you name Renoa the Dollmage and give her all your powers, they will treat both girls the same. Just in case."

I said, "That is probably wise," but it angered me to think people doubted me. To spite Mabe, I made a play doll for Annakey as well. Out of my scrap barrel, I made a hasty creation with a painted face and mitten hands and plain pajamas. Then, because Vilsa had passed me in the village that day without greeting me, I painted on its face a frown.

Some of the stucco had peeled off Vilsa's house, exposing the mud and lath beneath, but the ridges of turf that separated Vilsa's land from the other had been planted bright with daisies and poppies. Vilsa was out of doors, busy tanning a fleece and rendering mutton fat for the wick that winter.

Annakey saw what was in my hands and ran to me, perhaps hoping that I was bringing her Nesbeth.

"Here, child," I said, offering her the doll. "It is a gift for you, because you have been clever enough to live to be eleven years old."

"Mama says it is because of her wheat bread and not because I am clever. May I please have the doll anyway?"

She took the doll in her arms, saw the frown, and smiled.

She might have done nothing worse to fuel my resentment and wound my pride. Was I not Dollmage? Was I not supposed to be the wisest in the village?

Vilsa came and put her arm around Annakey.

"Annakey, you must thank Dollmage," she said simply.

Annakey laughed. "Thank you, Dollmage. Look Mama, my baby frowns. She must be tired, or hungry. . . ." She wandered away from the door, cuddling the doll, absorbed by its painted face.

"Are you teaching her to be a good wife?" I asked Vilsa.

She nodded. "She learns quickly." Vilsa was one of those who is more beautiful when not smiling.

"Good, because she will not be Dollmage."

Vilsa tilted her head to one side. "So you have said." It seemed to please her that I felt I must say it again. With great irritation I noticed her cheese press was scrubbed and polished.

"It is time for you to don widow's dark," I said.

"My husband is not dead."

"He is dead."

She looked at me long, then. "How can you know, unless the valley doll you made is . . ." Her face softened. "Dollmage, forgive me, but the valley doll you made for my husband—was there no power in it? Do not fear to tell me. I will forgive you."

The gall rose into my throat. Nothing will make one anger more quickly than being forgiven. "How dare you question me?" I said.

She did not answer. She looked long into my face, and I could see in her eyes that there was more than a drop of my grandmother's blood in her.

"Thank you for the gift you have given my daughter,

Dollmage," Vilsa said to me evenly. "Good night." She closed the door slowly and softly.

AFTER THAT DAY I RARELY SLEPT WELL. When I woke the next morning, the weight of the day was a comfort compared to the dreams that had pinned me to my pillow. I decided it was Vilsa's fault. When her cow died of the bloat that spring, I forbade the villagers to give her a widow's allotment. "She would be offended since she believes she is not a widow," I said. The following year I made sure all the sick and feeble had more than enough firewood for the winter. There was little left for Vilsa and Annakey. "Annakey is young and strong," I said. "Let her chop."

I hated to go into my secret, locked room. When I did, I would furtively bring out a piece of the broken valley doll and throw it in the trash. Soon there was not any of it left, but still I could not sleep. One day, I arose before dawn to walk away my bad dreams. As the sun lightened the sky, I stopped behind the shed. I thought I had seen my husband. He was not there, but in the faint light I saw footprints in the soft soil of the path. Worse, the ax had been moved from its usual place. Had he found his way out of the forest to come and cut my kindling for me? It would be so like him. But the dreams of the night pushed in on my waking a moment later, for I saw a black feather in the path, a message from the robber people.

The robber people had taken my ax.

It meant I was losing the power to make the story of my village, and for the first time in my life, I feared for my people.

[Chapter 4]

INSCRIPTION ON THE PLANTING CALENDAR DOLL:
Rutabagas are the key to happiness.

I HID THE BLACK FEATHER so as not to alarm the village. The next morning, while the light was new and sideways, I went to summon Renoa to my house.

The clouds pinked up as I walked the path between the trees. In the clearing my shadow stretched out long and thin. I crossed the river and saw the waterbugs pluck at the water, and butterflies the color of new green leaves fly from under the bridge where they slept. No one could know by the beauty of the day that the robber people had discovered our valley. Because my house was farthest away from the other houses of the valley, because it was alone in the trees, the robber people had first come there. It was a precious thing to take, my ax, for it had belonged to my husband's grandfather, but I knew from stories my grandmother told me of the other village that the ax would be only the beginning. The robber people are a cowardly people and would be timid at first. First they would steal an ax, then food from the gardens and sheds, then a cow. One day a woman would be gone, never to appear again, then children. The fear I felt as a child when my grandmother told me the stories returned to me now in my old age.

At the Willowknots' house Renoa was peeling rutabagas.

"I need Renoa to come with me," I said to Mabe.

"When she is done her work," Mabe said. We had begun to despise one another. Mabe saw that I was causing dissension among her daughters by telling Renoa that she would be the village storymaker, that hers would be a life of seeing and making, far above her sisters who would labor all their lives in kitchens and gardens and fields. For my part, I felt to inspire Renoa to show her talent. Today, however, I had no heart to offend Mabe further and so I said, "Come, Renoa, when you are done your work."

"No, Dollmage Hobblefoot," Renoa said. "I would go with you now. I shall destroy my hands on these thick peelings."

"Do as your mother says," I answered.

Renoa was appalled. It was the first time I had upheld her mother's decision. One of her sisters laughed low from a corner of the house, and Renoa's eyes slid from me to her mother to her sister. She went back to her peeling, but before I was out the door Renoa's sister cried aloud. I turned to see blood dripping from Renoa's hand.

"I told you I should destroy my hands if I were made to do such work. My hands are for dollmaking," Renoa said calmly.

Mabe's skin went the color of the rutabaga. Her mouth would not close.

"It is not so bad," I said to Mabe, thinking that she was fearful of the blood. "She will come with me, and I will bandage it." Mabe's fear was not assuaged by my words.

"Do you not see, Dollmage Hobblefoot? She draws her own blood to have her way," Mabe said. She said it wonderingly, as if she had not given birth to the girl herself.

"Is this true?" I asked Renoa. "Did you cut yourself intentionally?"

She did not answer. She drew herself up tall and looked at her mother, defying her. I bound her hand myself, in silence, and a little roughly. After that day, Mabe Willowknot had little to do with disciplining her daughter. She became mine.

To punish Renoa I said, "Now we will fetch Annakey." I said it also to arouse Renoa's jealousy, to provoke her to study and work. I did not think of Annakey. God has since forgiven my ignorance, but punished me for my selfishness. That is the way he has always loved me.

"Why must she come?" Renoa asked.

"Because you are too lazy and willful to be Dollmage."

"You are willful."

"I am. And I will that Annakey come."

"Why do you not name me the Dollmage?"

"When I do so, I will relinquish all my power. The villagers will need you to do the work of the Dollmage. You cannot work if you are off playing in the mountains."

Renoa answered nothing. Even as she walked beside me, her heart was upon the mountain. I knew it. I had been grateful for it until now. As long as she was unnamed, I could delay my promise to go with my husband. Now, however, I was afraid. I walked resolutely to Annakey's house, glad for Renoa's sour face.

We found Annakey, already finished breakfast and bent over a blanket she was stitching.

She stood up. "There. It is done. See, Dollmage, what I have made."

I could not help gasping.

The blanket was sky blue, with a yellow sun and pink and white clouds. Charming, but nothing that could not be done by another girl her age. What was startling was that there were birds embroidered into the sky. They were so cleverly sewn that one could distinguish what kind of bird each was, though none were bigger than my thumbnail: a plump robin, a bit-o'-sky, a jay, a dove, a thrush, a sparrow, a roof swallow, and a mill-thief. There were wild birds of the forest, tiny and perfect: quail, hawks, larks, and eagles. There was an entire flock of blackbirds. The blanket had been bordered in a darker blue, with tiny stars, and at the corners were clever moons in their stages. It had been made from scraps of yarn that others did not want. On the other side of the blanket was a worn, gray flannel lining. "For fog," Annakey said, laughing.

"What have you done?" I said to Vilsa.

She said, "You told me to teach her the womanly arts."

Renoa stared at the blanket and then at Annakey.

"It is a wonder," I said sincerely, then. My admiration overcame my anger. God was right in giving Annakey the totem of a Dollmage, for in her hands it seemed there was skill. Nevertheless, the gift, I knew, was with Renoa. I knew this because of the beggar doll Renoa had made, and the worry doll she had helped to make. I knew this because I fed upon her power to do my work.

"My mother helped," Annakey said, smiling at my praise. It was easy to see that her work had brought her much joy.

"I need Annakey to come with me," I said to Vilsa. Her eyes asked for explanation, but I offered none.

"Dollmage," Renoa said, "I want a blanket like this one."

Ah, I thought, at last she is showing a desire to create in miniature.

"You will have to study it, to know how it was done, Renoa," I said, smiling at her.

She frowned. "I want you to make it for me."

"I can teach you," Annakey said to Renoa.

"I cannot sew such things. My hands are made only for dollmaking," Renoa said, and her voice was not dismayed but sharp. She glared at Annakey.

Annakey studied her hands and then looked at me. "I, too, want to make the beautiful things that you make, Dollmage."

Renoa knew that Annakey had the promise doll of a Dollmage. She also knew that Annakey's promise doll had a frown where hers had a smile, and that Annakey's doll hung crookedly where hers hung straight. She had not feared that Annakey would have any power.

Now she looked at the charming sky blanket and for the first time she wondered if Annakey would not compete for her place as Dollmage. "The gift of dollmaking is not for you, but for me," she said.

"You have not yet been named Dollmage," Vilsa said quietly.

"She has a frowning promise doll. Mine smiles. Dollmage, I want a blanket just like this one. I want it, I want it." She started to cry. "I hate her," she said more quietly.

Vilsa's face was pale, as if her whole soul was clenched in a fist. I saw her look from Renoa's promise doll, to Annakey's, then to her own. She placed her fingers lightly on her own promise doll and closed her eyes briefly.

"Annakey," she said, "give Renoa the blanket."

There was a silence in the room. The fire settled.

Annakey clutched the blanket. "Mama, no," she said, so softly I barely heard.

"You see how Renoa weeps for it," Vilsa said gently.

"It is mine," Annakey said, more loudly now. She did not take her eyes away from her mother's.

"It would make her happy to have it. But it would make you happier still to give it. Do you understand, Annakey?"

Annakey shook her head and clutched the blanket close.

"Will you trust me?" Vilsa asked.

Annakey shook her head again, but her grip on the blanket loosened a little.

"You can make another blanket, Annakey," her mother said. "But you may never get another chance to do so generous a thing for Renoa."

"But, perhaps later, after I have slept with it one night?"

Her mother did not answer, but clutched her promise doll.

Annakey stared at Renoa with a frozen face. Finally, shaking, she slowly held out the blanket. Renoa snatched it with a cry of delight. She danced around the room with it. Annakey did not speak or move for a moment. Her face was blotched as if she had been struck.

"Can I keep it?" Renoa asked, not of Annakey but of me.

"Yes," Annakey said. She said it breathlessly, as if she had fallen into a winter river. "It is for you, Renoa, for you, who will one day be my Dollmage."

Renoa held the blanket to her as if she thought Annakey would change her mind and take it away.

I had disliked Vilsa before, but now I felt contempt for her. It seemed obvious to me that she hoped to ingratiate the future Dollmage to her daughter, and I thought it cruel of her to make Annakey give up the wondrous blanket. Is it not curious how we can justify only our own cruelties? I held my tongue, however, for Annakey was not smiling now, and that put my mind at peace.

The peace was short-lived. Slowly Annakey did begin to smile again, and more and more, until her whole face shone like polished porcelain. She turned to her mother. "You are right, Mama. It is in the making, not the having, that I was happy," Annakey said. She turned back to Renoa. "And in the giving."

Only then did I realize what Vilsa had done. She had not done it to ingratiate Renoa to her daughter. She had taught Annakey how to have a happiness that is beyond making oneself happy.

I saw that it had cost Vilsa. Her eyes were more shadowed with sadness, and her hand trembled as she bade Annakey good-bye.

IT WAS THE FIRST TIME Annakey had been in my house, and she was stupid with wonder. She could barely listen to my words, so taken was she with the dolls that hung from the rafters and the curios on the shelves and the stuff upon my tables. She held her arms stiffly, forbidding herself to touch, though Renoa carelessly picked up this bauble and that brightly colored ribbon, and tossed them back on the table. I was seduced by Renoa's confidence, whereas Annakey's respect made me want to be lordly in her eyes. I resisted, as any good Dollmage would do. I bade them both to come into another room of my house.

"You have long wanted to see what lies behind this door, Renoa," I said. "Now you shall see."

"And shall she see, also?" Renoa said, pointing to Annakey with one hand and clutching the sky blanket with the other.

"Yes," I said. We spoke to each other and did not look at Annakey.

I opened the door.

The girls looked. There were shelves on three walls of the room, and on them were Sacred dolls, filled with the lore and wisdom of our people. In the middle of the room was a large, round table, and on the table was a model of Seekvalley.

It was easily immediately recognizable as our village, so true was the replica, complete with a painted river, tiny models of each bridge and house, and trees to represent the wood. Renoa looked and then looked around, as if to say that this was not enough to be kept secret in another room. She went back to examining her blanket. Annakey swallowed the sight with her eyes, raised her hands as if she could not keep them from touching it, then folded them over her breast.

"These are the Sacred dolls," I said, gesturing to the shelves holding them. "As Dollmage, I care for them, study them, guard the stories that are hidden in them. See. Here is the Charter doll, with a scroll in it, describing the limits of each family's land. Here is the War doll. It is all right to fear it. I, too, am afraid when I look at it. Here is the Calendar doll, and here, most sacred, the God doll. Someday, Renoa, when you are Dollmage, you may study the scrolls hidden in them. By them and by the laws written there, will you guide and judge our people."

"Who made them?" Annakey asked softly.

"Certain great Dollmages have added to them over the ages. There have been many Dollmages, but few have made a doll worthy of becoming a Sacred doll. Not even I have done so, nor will I now in my old age." I swept my arm toward the table. "On the table is our village doll. No house is built in Seekvalley until it is first made here in miniature. No bridge is built until it is first fashioned for the village doll. I am the storymaker. I make the story of the village. It is the most important part of my work as a Dollmage. Look."

I took a bucket of water and poured it over the center of the village. All the water ran to the rivers and flowed off the doll. Annakey laughed with delight, but Renoa shrugged. "It is nothing more than what I have seen from the heights of the mountains," she said.

Annakey looked at the blanket Renoa was tightly clutching. "Renoa's blanket is like a doll of the sky," she said, smiling, as if she had just figured out the rules of an intricate game. We ignored her.

"Here is my house," Renoa said, poking at one of the tiny houses.

"Renoa, be gentle and pay attention," I said. "I will tell you what no one else in the village can know, and the reason why I brought you here. Last night I found a black feather behind my shed."

"Black?" Renoa said.

"Black."

"It was blue. Your eyes are old."

"It was black."

"Someone is playing a trick on you because you are a rude old woman."

"My ax is gone."

Renoa grimaced as if she had just bitten into a sour apple.

"It is your husband playing tricks on you."

"My husband is dead."

"I see his ghost sometimes."

I smiled a fleeting smile. "In the woods you see him," I said, "not in the village."

She did not argue.

I fetched the feather and held it before her eyes. "We have been found," I said.

I could see her remembering all the stories she had heard concerning the robber people. "Why have the robber people found us?" She said it shrilly. "It is your job as Dollmage to hide us."

I covered my chin to hide my shame. "That is one reason why the village doll stays here, locked in this dark room, away from all eyes but mine. It is to hide us from the robber people. But they have found us. It is no secret that I am old and my power is worn out. Renoa, you must find within yourself the power to help us."

"What can I do?" Renoa asked crossly. "You have not taught me well."

"You blame me? You have not listened well."

"You are boring."

"You are lazy!"

Renoa was weeping with fear and rage now. "I can do nothing when you are around me. You draw all the power from me. I can only feel it when I am far away from you, high in the mountains. . . ."

"You have not studied well. You have not been willing. Now something must be done, immediately."

Annakey, so taken with the village doll, had scarcely been listening. Now, during a pause of silence in our bickering, she said, "If I had not given my sky blanket to Renoa, I would cover the village with it. I would put the sky side down so that we would still see the sun, and the fog side being up would hide our village from the robber people."

It was a moment before I listened to what what my ears had heard. I turned slowly away from Renoa and looked at Annakey. Then I looked at the blanket. I looked at the village doll, and back again at the blanket. Renoa must have read my face, for she balled her sky blanket close to her heart.

"No," she said.

"Yes," I said.

"No!"

"Renoa," I explained as patiently as I could, "do you want the robber people creeping around your bed at night? They steal more than axes and chickens, you know. Have you not heard the tales?"

"My sisters frightened me with tales when I was little. I am no longer little," she said.

"No, you are not. Could you not do, then, as Annakey did, and give up something for the good of another? For the good of the village?" My voice was not so soft as Vilsa's had been. Renoa did not move. "You will do as I say, Renoa. You will put the sky blanket on the village doll."

Her eyes were as hard as the painted eyes of the Justice doll. At last, slowly, she put the blanket over the village doll. I looked to see if the same happiness that had been in Annakey's eyes was in her own. I could not see it.

"There," she said. "I have saved the village."

"I don't know," I said. "It might work. But if it does, it is Annakey that has saved the village, is it not? She made the blanket." I said it to punish Renoa for resisting me.

Renoa glared at Annakey as if she had said those words, and not I. "In her hands is skill," Renoa said, "but it is my hands that placed it over the village. In my hands is the power."

THREE DAYS LATER, I knew it had worked. No one complained that they were missing anything, and I found no more black feathers. The blanket had changed the story of the village. The robber people might have forgotten about us, or been frightened off by some sign or omen, or perhaps the one who stole the ax died before he could bring it back to his people. In any case the sky blanket had saved our village for a time and had given me time to teach the young Dollmage.

I forbade Annakey to speak of anything she had seen in my house. Now I will tell you what I could not know if it were not that Annakey makes this story. When she arrived home, her mother asked her a question.

"Annakey, did you see the new valley doll that Dollmage made before you were born? Did you see it safe? Did you see the man doll in it? That is your father."

Annakey obeyed my injunction not to speak, but remembered that she had seen nothing of a new valley doll. She never forgot about the man doll.

RENOA RETURNED TO HER EXPLORING and Annakey returned to her work. Vilsa was often weak and her mind adrift. It was for Annakey to milk the goat and churn the cream, to harvest the garden and dry it, to kill the chicken and roast it. She learned to card and spin, weave and knit, and tan hides. She could shear a sheep, deliver a lamb, and cook a mutton stew. Even so, she was often seen making shawls for old people, and mittens and hats for children. All were embroidered in the finest detail with birds and animals and flowers. In spite of her frowning promise doll, people regarded the embroidery with wonder and asked among themselves, "Can Renoa do such things with her hands?"

Finally I realized what was happening. "You must no longer embroider," I told her.

"But what harm . . . ?"

"It is too much like the Dollmage's art," I said.

She stopped. She did not know anymore what to do with her hands when they were not working. Sometimes I saw her hands twitch and squeeze, but only for a few days did she forget to smile. Her persistent cheer was enough to make me take to my bed. Can you blame me for disliking the girl?

NO, I SEE YOU DO NOT BLAME ME, you who think to punish Annakey for the fate that has come to our village. She broke her promise and brought God's wrath upon us, you say. You refuse to loosen the ropes at her ankles, though they have become wet with blood. Only touch the memory dolls I gave you to your foreheads and you will remember that you liked her then.

I INSISTED THAT ANNAKEY come to my house almost every day to do me some small service.

"If you had time for handwork, you have time to help an old woman," I said.

She swept my floors, washed pots, dusted, scrubbed, and tidied. Her mother had taught her well. I forbade her to touch any of the doll stuff, but I could not stop her from looking. How she looked. How she strained to watch me a little if I was working. She would do anything to sneak peeks as I made dolls. For a time I suffered it, until one day she asked, "Dollmage, where is my father's doll?"

It took the breath out of me, as if she had struck me.

Finally I said, "He is where he should be." I bade her leave. She must have felt my anger, for she did not speak of it again.

One day in winter, when the mountain paths were snowed in, Renoa came into the house and began playing with the material on the table and in the baskets.

"Dollmage does not let us touch," Annakey said, watching Renoa handle the doll stuff the way a starving man watches bread being sliced and buttered.

"She lets me," Renoa said. I was standing in the room and did not contradict Renoa. Annakey stood still a moment, the broom in her hand, watching as Renoa worked more earnestly with the doll stuff than she ever had before.

"Do you not have work to do?" I asked Annakey. I was pleased whenever Renoa showed an interest, even if it had begun as a desire to taunt Annakey.

"No, Dollmage, I am done," she said. She was not smiling, and so my heart softened.

"Not done. Please sweep the room that houses the village doll, only you must not touch it."

Annakey went about her work. As soon as Annakey was out of sight in the other room, Renoa ran away. I called out to her, but she did not listen. She ran to the feet of Mount Lair where she played as wild as a deer fawn. In a little while, Annakey came to me with the dustpan. She was staring into it.

"Look, Dollmage," she said. "Look what I found on the floor."

My stomach sickened at the sight. It was one of the men I had made for the new valley doll that I had broken and thrown away. It had been in a dusty corner of the room all these years, a little piece of a story I had not been able to make.

"Who is it?" Annakey asked.

"Never mind," I said. "You should not have found this." I took the man piece and threw it out the window to the chickens. "Now go away, and do not come back. I told you not to touch anything. And never tell your mother about this."

Annakey stared out the window after the man doll, and then looked at me a long moment. Her arms hung still at her sides. Did she guess what I had done? Perhaps she hoped that her fears were for nothing.

"I will go," she said. She made as if to walk away, then stopped. "Dollmage, you must let me come back."

"Do not tell me what I must do," I said, turning away from her.

"Dollmage, I have such longings inside me for the things

of your art. I think of it all the time. I dream of things I could make, beautiful things. . . ." She blushed to hear herself say it. Her voice lost its pleading edge. "The village is growing, the men say. Perhaps Renoa will need help when she is Doll-mage. Perhaps there is some gift in my hands also."

I did not answer. Still she was not discouraged. She stepped closer to me.

"Dollmage, I feel something in me. . . . As soon as I saw the Sacred dolls, I felt it."

Her tone moved me to wonder if I had made an error. Renoa was wild and haughty. Annakey was skilled and kind. Then I remembered that around her neck hung the frown-ing promise doll. Suddenly, her presence pained me like a tooth that aches at sweets.

"If you revere the Sacred dolls, then listen to what they say, Annakey Rainsayer: There cannot be two Dollmages in a vil-lage. Never two."

"Then perhaps I am the one." She said it quietly, but as if she had wanted to say it all her life.

I sighed. "You must accept, Annakey. Your promise doll frowns."

"But what if it means something else? Are you sure that the frowning doll means that I will not be Dollmage?"

Now she was behaving like her mother, questioning my art. "Would I not know the meaning of the work of my own hands?"

If she heard the edge in my voice it did not deter her. "Mother says there may be more than one meaning—"

"Enough."

"She says we may make things mean what we will—"

"Leave!" I said. She started at the anger in my voice, as if it had not been there all along.

If she made the smallest sound as she left I did not hear it. My hand grasped the edge of the table beside me and I bent over it to keep myself from falling. If I was wrong, if things did not mean what they meant, if I could not make the story of the village without it turning and making me, then the whole world was upside down and I could barely hold on.

I WENT TO BED FOR SEVERAL DAYS, and when I got up I went to the river for a walk. The young people played at the river. Annakey did her mother's wash a little way downstream. I had been right about the way Vilsa raised Annakey. She was dismayed by the way the other young ones played, teasing and arguing and pinching each other. When she finished the wash, she went off a little by herself. She glanced about her to see if anyone was watching and then began taking bits of clay from the shallows of the river. Almost without thinking, it seemed, she began fashioning the clay into tiny replicas of animals—a chicken, a dog, a bird, a rabbit. Her hands were deft, her movements graceful as if it were an ecstasy to her, and she worked the clay masterfully. I should have run to her, punished her, but I could not take my eyes away.

Manal on silent feet came up behind Annakey and he too became entranced as he watched her work the clay. Annakey was disappointed with her first efforts and began again, this time making a pig. Manal laughed to see the exactness with which she reproduced the animal.

"You have made a pig exactly like the pig my uncle slaughtered this fall," he said.

"I hate the fall slaughter," Annakey said.

"And I," answered Manal. "When I am grown I will be a hunter instead. That way the animal will have a chance to run away."

Annakey smiled, and then frowned. "This pig is not very good," she said. She squeezed the clay together and began again. This time she made a cow, and it was all I could do not to come from my hiding spot and look at it more closely. Manal thrilled to see it. He laughed out loud.

Renoa and her friends Willa and Hasty came to see what Manal's laughter was about. Areth came too. Everyone but Renoa laughed delightedly to see the cow, so like a cow in every detail.

"Look, Renoa, it is your mother's cow Rolly. It has the same crooked tail," Willa said. Her smile faded when she looked at Renoa's face. They were used to Renoa's tempers, but never had they seen her face so green, so aghast, so enraged. A moment later her face relaxed, but her eyes were as dull as if they were painted on.

"I can do that, too, of course," Renoa said. "Only better."

"Yes, better," Willa and Hasty chimed in.

Areth looked away and his smile faded.

"I have never seen you do it," Manal challenged.

Renoa picked up a piece of damp clay and fashioned it into a deer.

"Oh, Renoa," Willa said.

"It is good," Manal said grudgingly, "but not better than Annakey's." He was an ear of corn, covered by a tough husk, underneath sweet and tender.

Renoa looked from one set of eyes to another, then reached for Annakey's cow and threw it in the river.

"Come here, all of you," Renoa said after a moment. The others gathered around Renoa quickly. Manal stayed seated, but Annakey stood up, glad that Renoa did not appear to be angry anymore. "Not you," Renoa said to Annakey, and then she beckoned to Manal. "Come listen, and I will tell you about a party I am going to have."

Manal did not move. Finally Renoa moved away, chattering, and the group, including Areth, followed her. Once they stopped, looked back at Annakey, and laughed together. Areth's face went red with shame, shame that he allowed the group to taunt Annakey, shame also that he was her friend.

They were too far away for Annakey to hear what was being said. She turned and ran away.

Manal called after her, but she did not hear. She could only hear the laughter of the others, and her own mind telling her a hundred reasons why they were justified in despising her.

I knew I must speak to Renoa. A terrible thing is a Dollmage without compassion for her people. Can you not see that by observing me? Some part of me was secretly glad at what had happened. I had placed a frown on Annakey's promise doll, but never was there a child who smiled so much. Now, I thought, somewhere in the bad bits of my brain, she had finally lost her smile. Still, I meant to punish Renoa. No sooner had I emerged from my hiding place to do so than Areth Lowmeadow came running to me, the dust flying around him.

"Dollmage! Dollmage! Come quick. Mabe Willowknot's cow has fallen into the river and is like to drown."

"Rolly?"

"Yes. Come."

It was too late. The cow's leg was broken in the fall and she drowned. I found Renoa standing on the bank. She was old enough to understand the great hardship it would be to her family to lose their milk cow.

"Annakey did this, Dollmage Hobblefoot. She made a clay cow just like Rolly, and . . ."

"And . . . ?"

She stared up at me. "I threw it in the river." She looked at her hands as if they were not her own.

"So who has the power, Renoa? Is it Annakey who made the cow, or yourself who threw it in the river?"

"Annakey must pay," she said bitterly.

"To ask her to pay will convince the villagers that it was all her doing. They will wonder if you are indeed the true Dollmage. Need we complicate this matter?"

She thought a moment. "No."

"Then hush."

"Teach me, Dollmage."

"I will begin to teach you tomorrow. Finally you have shown a desire. It is what I have been waiting for."

Renoa smiled.

I said, "It will be hard for your mother without her cow. I am sorry."

"Perhaps it would be better if I came and lived with you," she said. "Then my mother would not need as much milk and cheese."

And so it was that out of a bad thing came that which was good. As for Annakey, out of a bad thing came that which was even worse.

Manal and the other children told their parents what had happened. Some of you believed that the power was in Annakey's hands and not Renoa's. A small delegation of you came to my house a few nights after Renoa had moved into my house.

"The young ones say it was Annakey that fashioned the doll of Rolly," Ham Wifebury said. "Could it be that she and not Renoa is the Dollmage to come after you?"

"Her promise doll has the eyes of a Dollmage, so it is reasonable to think that she has a small power," I said. "But you see what becomes of the use of her power." I softened my voice, knowing that my words had already recreated Annakey in your minds. "She is only a child. It is not her fault. It is God's Fault. Capital *F*. What else can we expect from someone with a frowning promise doll?"

Everyone was frowning after I said that, as you are frowning now. Do you not see how I planted the seed of your hatred?

"But what does the frown mean?" Ham asked.

"As I said, it means she will not be Dollmage."

"Are . . . are you . . . s-sure?" he stammered. "Perhaps—"

"It was Renoa who threw the cow in the river. It is her hands that made the end of the story for Rolly." I said it sharply. "If Renoa hadn't done it herself, she would have tried to get payment from Annakey."

This quieted them until Manal said, "What of the deer that Renoa made? Was there any power in that?"

"See for yourself," I said, gesturing toward the gloom of the trees behind my house. There Renoa frolicked with a small deer, teasing it with sweet flowers. The day after Rolly drowned she had found it in the forest, left motherless by wolves. It became her pet. The men watched as the young deer ate salt out of her pocket.

They left, but not before Manal said, "If Annakey has even a small power, should it not be trained and under your eye?" Because his father was dead and he did the work of a grown man, he had the vote of an adult.

I bent my head. "Thank you for helping me to see this. She will be ever under my eye."

You thought I was humble, but in truth I was only saying I would watch Annakey more closely, that she might not cause any more trouble. I felt it my place to care for you in this way.

"Words are like dolls," Renoa said later when I told her what the men had said. "They make things happen."

"Now you begin to see," I said.

I took the God doll down from the shelf in the other room and took the parchment out of its hiding place. "'Words are God's dolls,'" I read. "'With a word he made us. Only to us, his children, did he give words and the power to make.' That is why the promise is so important. If we break a promise, a word means nothing, and if a word means nothing, then we have lost the power God gave us."

"But . . . but with that power came the freedom to lie, the ability to destroy a real thing with words," Renoa said. You see how clever she was at a young age.

"Yes. That is why we have promise dolls, to watch our words, and to help us keep the promise that God placed in us. Now here is our power: to make the story of our village by the art of our hands. Dollmage is storymaker. Through the eyes of the Dollmage is the story told."

Renoa looked at me boldly and as an equal. "Yes, I begin to see."

I picked up a carving knife and a piece of wood and began to teach her, but my old hands shook and I could not think why.

[Chapter 5]

INSCRIPTION ON THE LULLABY DOLL:
Promise doll, do not weep,
This promise I must keep.

Promise doll, do not sleep,
This promise I will keep.

As I SAID, Annakey ran away when Renoa led the other young people to taunt her. Now I will tell you where Annakey ran. How do you know, Dollmage? you ask with your eyes. How can you tell us the truth about Annakey, where she went and what she thought? The children know, but I forbid them to tell. Believe me only when I tell you that the Dollmage is the storymaker. Listen to me then, as the children do.

Annakey ran alongside the river until the houses were all past her. She ran until there were no more bridges, until the fields turned to thorn and thicket, and on until the underbrush turned to saplings and the saplings to shadowed forest. She ran until she came to where the river comes fast out of the mountain. It is a feared place. Here the bear and the cougar come to water and the wolves come to howl. Here the great trees have spirits and hang down their long branches to pinch and scratch. Here there are eyes in every hole. Annakey did not care that cougars and bears had lapped at the water, nor that there were bones in the shallows.

Annakey is afraid of only one thing, and that is not it.

Look into her eyes now. Though you keep your stones hard by your sides, though you wish to have my tale over so you can execute her, there is no fear in her eyes. No, Annakey is afraid of only one thing.

What is it, the children ask. I will not tell you now. Later. My temper is frayed from sleeping in the open last night. It is a wonder you do not wear out your voices, snoring all night. So many snores! It is useful for keeping the bears and wild-cats away at night, but hard on a Dollmage's temper.

As I was saying, Annakey sat on a rock at the riverbank and listened to the sound of the rushy water. I will tell you what Annakey learned as she sat upon that rock.

First, Annakey learned that morning to be alone. That is a great power.

Second, she learned that there is cruelty in the world. She did not yet understand that those who hurt others do so because they believe that people desire to hurt them. She did not know yet that such people suffer more than the ones they hurt, for they must live in their own skin, in a world of their own making, a world full of enemies. Annakey would be years older before she learned this, but today she had learned about cruelty. That lesson in itself was valuable.

Annakey did not appreciate the lesson. Her throat and chest ached. The flat rock she lay on absorbed the heat of the sun, but Annakey felt the cold of its heart. Icy water slicked the rocks in the shallows. After a long time she noticed that in the river shallows was a patch of clay. It was clean and slippery, pale green in color. She dug at it with her fingers, retrieved a handful, and began to work it. She made a sheep.

The pain in her throat and chest began to diminish.

For the first time Annakey looked at her surroundings and found that it was a wondrous place. The trees were thick all around, but had backed away to make a small, round clearing by the river. The grass was thick and soft here, not too high, and scented with bee-lace and mud orchids. The trees hung their branches over the clearing protectively. Even the water was tamer here, eddied into a quiet little bay at the foot of the large, flat rock that Annakey was sitting on. It charmed her. It was like a little room in the woods just for her. There was even a hidey-hole, for one of the trees had a huge knot in its trunk. She put the clay sheep in the knothole, but there would be enough room to hide more treasures if she were to come here again.

WHEN ANNAKEY RETURNED to the village and learned that Rolly the cow had drowned, she came to me, her face the color of the pale green clay under her fingernails.

"I drowned Rolly," she said. "I will pay."

"You made the doll, but Renoa threw it in the river. It is prideful to think you did it, to think you have the power."

Annakey looked down at her hands, relieved that they had done nothing appalling and without her permission. Only then did she think to blush under my rebuke.

"Nevertheless," I said, "you must promise me that you will not make any more such animal dolls. I have told the villagers I will watch you."

She nodded. A nod is as good as a promise.

After a few days, she noticed that some people would no longer speak to her as she went about her work, and those who did spoke to her differently than before. Still Annakey smiled, but oh, such tucking away of bitterness there must have been.

At the end of the day, Annakey returned to her hiding place. She brought with her an old wool blanket so dense it could keep out a morning's rain. She brought dried fruit and a fishhook, a spoon, a pot, a small box of oil, and salt. Carefully she took her clay sheep out of the knothole and laid it on the large, flat rock by the river.

She gathered moss for a lawn for the clay sheep to eat in. She found pebbles for boulders and bits of pine for bushes and small-leafed twigs for great trees. She fashioned a shallow bowl of clay and filled it with water for a pond. She broke bits of her hair to float in the pond for fishes. Tiny bluebells and baby's breath that she found growing wild on the riverbank were sweet flowers for her sheep in his meadow. She kept her promise to me, however, that she would not make any more animal dolls. Her sheep had the meadow to himself.

When Annakey returned home she did her work with a song and a light hand. Even when the work became heavy and long, when the other children played while Annakey must weed and clean and cook, she had a meadow for her mind to live in.

BECAUSE OF HER PET DEER, Renoa's desire to do the work of a Dollmage left her again. She would stay all day upon the mountain and come home only at dark. At times she slept in the woods. She took her friends from the village to places no one had seen. She became respected for her knowledge of the wilderness and all things in it.

I prayed for the day the deer would go wild again and leave her. Once I tried to take her clay deer from her pocket as she slept. I would put the doll over the mountains, far away from the Seekvalley village doll. But she woke, and her eyes glowed in the darkness like a wild animal's.

"What are you doing?" she whispered in the dark. Her

voice hissed low and piercing as a serpent's. I felt a chill between my shoulder blades.

"It is time for you to be a woman and do the work of a woman," I said, my voice just above a whisper.

"I will do my own work," she said.

"You will work here, with me."

"No." She was not arguing with me. She was explaining. "You suck the magic out of me, old woman. I feel my power only when I am far away from you."

"Renoa."

"Someday, when I am Dollmage, I will make new valleys and new mountains, and I will go there." Then she dressed herself and ran out of the house into the night.

She was fearless, and all my efforts to tame her only made her vicious.

I CEASED TO WORRY ABOUT ANNAKEY. She grew out of my sight and largely out of my mind. Over the next three years, her mother became weaker of body and mind, and rarely went out of doors. She did sewing and mending in exchange for the things she and Annakey could not provide for themselves. Annakey had to care for the cow and the pig and the chickens; she had to plant and weed and harvest the garden. She was too busy to trouble me. I did not know that whenever she could, she would run away to her secret place where the mountains' toes are bunched, where the sheep do not wander for fear of wolves and mountain cats. I did not know she would add to her meadow, putting in hedges and bees, and dew on the leaves, and all manner of wonders. I did not know what made her happy. I did notice that Oda Weedbridge's field was lusher that year, and that in it the wildflowers grew more abundantly than anywhere else in the valley. I spread dust over her field in the Seekvalley doll so it would not excite envy among the villagers, but it remained green and thick with flowers as ever. I could not know that already Annakey was stealing my story.

VILSA HAD A SECRET OF HER OWN. Whenever Annakey was gone, Vilsa had taken to spending her time in the root shed where she could think about her husband without interruption. She spoke to him while she was in there, laughing over old jokes they had shared and quietly swearing her love forever. Her grief had become madness. One day I listened at the window and heard her carrying on a conversation with her husband.

I looked in the window. "Vilsa," I said, "who are you speaking to?"

"My husband," she said.

"He is not here," I said.

"His ghost, then."

I looked all around. "His ghost is not here."

Vilsa looked around the room groggily, as if coming out of a trance. "No," she said. "He is not dead."

"If he is not dead, he does not love you enough to return to you. It is not my fault."

Of course it was my fault. I chose not to think of it, to delay the day of my repentance.

One day not long after that, Annakey summoned me to the house. She was dough-colored, and her eyes were swollen.

"Dollmage," she said. "Mother is ill."

"She is always ill."

"This time it is different," Annakey said.

"It comes of spending too much time in the root shed," I said sharply, but I followed her to the house.

When I arrived, I saw everything as usual. The windows were polished and the stoop swept. The laundry was hanging fresh, the lamp was trimmed, the butter churned and molded.

I looked at Vilsa and knew at once she was dying.

The woman looked away, staring at the mountains through her sparkling windows as if her husband might come for her even yet. She knew also.

"Take care of my daughter," she said weakly. "Teach her to use her gift."

"Renoa is the true Dollmage," I said. "It is possible that Annakey drowned a cow, but to tame a deer is the work of a Dollmage. You know the law. There cannot be two to a village."

Vilsa got up on one elbow. The effort made her forehead and chin glisten with sweat. "Listen, Grandmother Hobble-foot," she said. "You think my promise doll drained me of my happiness so that Annakey might have it. You are wrong. It is her promise doll that did it. She has great power to make the story go how she wills it. Teach her, Dollmage." She lay back on the pillows. "Care for her until her father returns for her."

She was again telling me my own art.

"If you insist her father lives, she will be denied an orphan's portion. But I will do my best to see that she is cared for."

Annakey knelt beside her mother. She was not smiling now. Her face was full of astonishment, as if she had never seen death before.

"Is it true, Mother? Did I take your happiness for my own? I will give it back."

Vilsa touched her daughter's hand. "Things have been as they were meant."

"I will make things to be as I wish them," Annakey said. She was weeping openly now.

"Someday you will understand about daughters, how their happiness becomes your own," Vilsa said.

"Are you afraid to die?"

"A little. You can help me to be less afraid."

"Tell me, Mama. I will do anything."

"Take your promise doll in your hand."

Annakey did so.

"Promise me, now, that you will be happy, that you will make your life good."

I gasped. "She will do no such thing. That is for God to decide."

"Promise me, child," Vilsa said. "It is my dying wish."

"I promise, Mother," she said.

Vilsa closed her eyes and her hands were still. "Tell your father," she whispered, "that I died speaking of my love for him." She looked out the window and I saw her smile for the first time in years.

Then she died.

Annakey moaned as if her stomach were in pain. She laid her head on her mother's chest.

"Come," I said.

"Dollmage Hobblefoot, I feel I am going to be sad forever," Annakey said, and in her face was real fear.

So. Finally. The promise doll I had made her was not without power after all.

"Come. I have an idea of someone who will take you in."

She closed her eyes. After a time she stood up. "No. I am not an orphan. I have a father yet, and I am old enough to live here on my own until he returns."

The way she said it made me look at her differently. I was astonished to realize how grown she was. She was as tall as I, and with the breasts of a woman. My Renoa was the same age, of course, but she seemed younger to me. By the time I was this age I was doing all the work of a full Dollmage. Renoa still dabbled and played, and had no taste for the labor.

"You'll get no orphan's portion unless you raise your father's tombstone along with your mother's," I said.

"My father promised my mother that he would return," she said. "If I give up on the promise he made, it will kill him. My faith will keep him alive. I will do extra work for my keep."

I thought of the smashed valley doll, its pieces long since broken beyond recognition, and I was sick with guilt.

"What will you do for work?" I demanded.

"I—I do not know. . . ."

"Have you manure shovels? Buckets?"

She shrugged, defeated.

"Come. I know who does." I grabbed her hand and pulled her out of the house.

THE TRUTH IS I BELIEVED I was God's defender. Was it not for him to decide who would be happy and who would not? Was it not for him to send the fruitful field, the long-milking cow and good health? If we lacked for anything, was it not God's Fault? Capital *F?* He it was who had given Annakey a frowning promise doll. I encouraged her promise doll to keep its promise by taking Annakey to work for the egg-woman.

The egg-woman was Oda Woodbridge. She was a spring berry, small and bright red, but so sour as to bring tears to the eyes. She lived at the far end of the village, in the last house, in fact, that Annakey would run past on the way to her secret place. She was a spinster who refused to accept the help due her from the village. She burned dried cow dung for fuel, saving for rainy days the little wood she could forage for herself.

She had worn the same dress for five years, and to cover it had made herself new aprons out of the scraps that others could not use. She ate from her own garden, and grew her own grain. What she could not grow or make herself, she bought with money she earned as the egg-woman.

Though everyone had their own chicken coop in their yard, few people looked forward to the task of entering the smelly coop to search for eggs. Oda did it every morning for people, and in return they let her keep an egg or two. Of course she could not consume that many eggs herself, and so she sold the rest to those whose chickens were not laying at the time. Oda was a proud woman even though she had great ugliness to keep her humble, and she became prouder as year after year she refused her due as a spinster. When I asked her why she would not take her spinster's allotment, she replied, "Because then I would have to be grateful, and that is more exhausting than work." She was wise in a sour sort of way.

"What have you brought her here for?" Oda said to me when I arrived at her door with Annakey.

"Vilsa died," I said. "She needs work."

"Give her the due of an orphan," Oda replied. "I have no work for her."

"She is not an orphan. Her father is alive, or so her mother claimed. She must work for her living."

"Again I ask: Why do you bring her to me? There are not enough eggs for two of us."

"Think, Oda, how much more money you could make if you could clean out the chicken coops for people."

"I am too old to clean out chicken coops," she said. She was an insufferably stubborn woman, but before she finished her sentence she understood what I was proposing. "Oh," she said. She looked at Annakey with interest.

"She needs the use of your shovels and buckets. You arrange the work with those of the village who are happy with your work as egg-woman. Make sure she does well, and take a portion of her pay."

Oda nodded, and that is how Annakey became the chicken-coop girl.

[Chapter 6]

INSCRIPTION ON THE STORY DOLL:
*Run away into a story, and when you
come out at the end you will find yourself
even closer to home.*

HARD WORK MAKES YOU LOSE your beauty if you are bitter,
but Annakey did not become bitter. It was tucked away too
far behind her heart, and had she not promised her mother
she would be happy? All of us watched as Annakey grew
more fair and true, careful in her speech, and faithful in keeping the promises to which she was born. She could not play
as the other village youth did, but she took satisfaction in
working hard. It was not only for her living. After all, Manal
brought her meats and fowls and she was not starved. No, she
needed to work to assuage the need in her heart to create in
miniature. This I know now. How her fingers wished to make
the world she saw. This, she would say with her fingers, this is
how my eyes see, this is how the world is real.

Not long after her mother died, she smiled. I began to
think she had no feeling, and I treated her so. One night she
drove me too far.

It was on a summer evening, when the sun had gone
behind the mountain but still filled the sky with light. I see it
even now by the power of the storymaker. It had been so hot
that summer that the waterslicks, usually wet with glacier
water, were as dry as tracks. The old people sat on their stoops

for relief and even the babies stayed up late, cooling their bottoms in the clover. The older boys were playing at chance-bones, gambling away their fathers' land by the foot for some day when it would be theirs alone. Manal sat apart, not gambling. Renoa had found it too hot to hike on the mountain so she stayed in the village with her friends. She and the girls approached the boys.

"Come play bat-the-barrel with us," Renoa said to the boys, her friends gathered behind her.

"There! I win. The east bush of your barley field is mine," Areth said to Dantu.

"Miller must first give me the marsh bottom at the end of his cow meadow," Dantu said.

Miller laughed. "You will first have to play or fight my brothers for it. They are so much older than I, they will have divided the land between their own sons by the time I am grown to claim it."

No one was looking at Renoa until she said, "By the time the land is divided between all of you, there will not be enough for you to have a wife, never mind sons of your own."

They all laughed but Manal, and his silence sobered them quickly. "Why do you laugh?" Manal said.

"What else can be done?" Areth said.

"When it comes to pass that there is not enough food, no one will laugh. Something could be done if a new valley was found."

"Dollmage says there are no new valleys," Renoa said, "but Dollmage has not walked to the top of Mount Crownantler and has not seen what I have seen, the world stretching away without end. . . ."

"Mountains," Areth said.

"But where there are mountains, there needs to be a valley," Manal said evenly.

All the eyes gazed toward the mountaintops with longing and fear. "Someday we will have to go," Manal said.

"That is a long time away," Areth said lightly.

"Yes. So come play bat-the-barrel with us," Renoa said, "and we promise we will eat very little when we are your wives."

Areth stood chuckling, but the other boys looked at Manal and did not move, waiting to see what he would do.

"Will you play, Manal?" Areth said.

Manal looked at something through the heat haze and the smoke of the common fire. "If Annakey can play," he said.

The smile remained on Renoa's lips but drained out of her eyes. "She is always too busy," she said.

"She will play," Areth said. "I will fetch her."

He brought her, almost dragging her by the hand to where the village youth were waiting. The boys stood when she came, and said hello and joked with her.

Renoa, in a loud voice, began outlining the farthest limits where one could hide, and how high the seeker had to count.

"Annakey, you can be the first seeker," Renoa said.

"You go first, Renoa," Manal said. "You are the one who wanted the game."

"I will," she said, with her doll's smile, and she began counting.

They played and hid and laughed in the deepening twilight, and on beneath the blurred stars. Each of the boys took turns having Annakey hide with them in their best spots, crouching close with her until they were found and had to race for the barrel. Manal seemed always close by, wherever she was hiding. Annakey forgot to be careful of Renoa and laughed outright, and for the first time that evening Manal laughed too.

Finally, it was Areth's turn to show Annakey his favorite hiding place, which was in the upper boughs of a tree. While they were hiding, Areth asked for a kiss.

Annakey shook her head and pointed to Tawm who was seeker, and coming close to them.

"Yes," Areth said.

"Shh," she said. "Here comes Tawm."

"Yes," Areth said again.

Annakey moved from the upper boughs to the lower boughs, her eyes on Tawm, ready to run and reach the barrel first if he spotted them.

"I will have a kiss," Areth said, coming close to her.

Annakey drew away. "A kiss is a kind of promise," she said, "to the one you will marry."

Areth grabbed her arm and held it tight. "Then promise to marry me."

Annakey laughed low, uncomfortably, thinking to make light of it. "We are not children," she said. Areth did not smile.

Annakey stopped pretending it was nothing. "No," she said, trying to pull her arm away.

Areth put his mouth close to her ear. "Your mother and father are dead. There is no one to protect you."

"You speak like a robber boy," Annakey said angrily.

"Seen! Seen!" Tawm called. Annakey was on the ground and running almost before he cried out. Areth was quick after her, but then Manal seemed to appear from nowhere. Annakey hit the barrel, gasping for air. She saw Manal exchange a word with Areth. Areth turned and went in the direction of home, and that is when he began to let winter live in his heart.

When everyone else had gathered around the barrel, Manal said, "It is too dark to play anymore. We must be up early for the fields."

"Once more," Renoa said.

"Yes, once more," the other girls said, except for Annakey, who had not learned how to follow Renoa.

The boys drifted away. "Good night, Annakey," some of them said, ignoring Renoa.

Renoa stared after them a moment. "We girls will play once more, then," she said at last. "Annakey, now you will be seeker."

The girls vanished into the shadows. Annakey counted and then began seeking. She was joyous. For the first time in a very long time, she had laid aside the burdens of an adult and played like a child. She looked behind the trees and in the bushes. She looked near the river, behind the boulders, among the village ovens still smelling of bread, and under the drying trays heavy with shriveled fruit. She looked in all the favorite hiding spots until the moon had ridden some of her slow arc across the stars.

She found no one.

Finally she called out: "I give up! Renoa! Hasty! Willa!"

There was no answer. Annakey waited, and then looked some more. She stood by the barrel until the common fire was no more than glowing ash. Finally, she heard a rustle in the grasses.

"Renoa?" Annakey said, smiling into the dark.

"It is me, Manal. I heard you calling."

"Manal, I cannot find any of them. Come, help me. . . ."

"They are not hiding," Manal said. "I saw them at Doll-mage's house. All of them."

Manal said nothing while Annakey realized that they had played a trick on her.

In the meantime, I had been treating Renoa and her friends to a hot barley drink on my stoop. At first I thought their laughter was high spirits, until I listened to their talk. I went to fetch Annakey myself. My heart could be kind toward her when I knew she was sad and frowning, but when I opened the door, I saw her walking home with Manal. He was saying such things as to make her smile despite her hanging head and drooping shoulders.

My pity drained away. Everything that made her sad found a way to lead to smiling, smiling, smiling.

ANNAKEY WAS SHOVELING MANURE in my chicken coop the next day.

"If your mother had not died, you would not have to work this way," Renoa said to her. "But then, she brought it on herself."

Annakey ignored Renoa and attended to her shoveling. She had learned over the years that it made her unhappier to fight back than it did to endure Renoa.

"Do you like to work for Oda the egg-woman?"

"She is very thrift," Annakey said after a moment.

"Dollmage says she will give me a toffee doll today when I have learned a few things," Renoa replied.

I called, "Come in, Renoa. It is time to work."

"Now, Dollmage Hobblefoot? It is such a beautiful day."

"Time is running short. I am old. If I died tomorrow, what would you do?"

"You won't die tomorrow, Grandmother. You are young and strong. Please, let me be with my friends just an hour longer and then we will begin." She was smiling at Annakey, and it made her voice sweet.

"Very well," I said. "You may have one more hour."

Renoa had learned already about armature, which is the frame or body core of a doll, made of metal or wire or wood. Later that day, when she had played a little, we would spend some time on pigments. I would teach her to bind it with egg white, and perhaps I would teach her how to make gall ink. Tomorrow I would teach her to make a peddler doll, with an apron full of pockets into which would go pins and buttons and small things. With a peddler doll, these important things would never get lost. Even if you mislaid them and forgot to put them back in the peddler doll's pockets, they would re-appear there. It was one of my favorite tricks of the trade.

Still later, Renoa would make a pauper doll, of rags and odds and ends, to remind her to be generous to the poor. After the pauper doll, I would teach her to make nesting dolls to give to a child who was not growing well. She could make a moss doll to give to a hunter so he would not get lost.

In my dreaming I did not hear what was going on in my own backyard until it was too late. Looking out I saw Renoa and several of her friends standing around the chicken coop, watching Annakey work. They were laughing at her.

Annakey took her shovelful of manure and dropped it on Renoa's feet. Then the girls were laughing at Renoa instead, and her face was blank with rage. Before I could poke my head out the window again, Renoa stepped forward and pushed Annakey into the muck. She pushed her so hard her whole body was covered. Even her hair dripped with chick-en manure.

Annakey was not smiling. For a moment she sat, stunned, in the manure. She moved her hand and seemed to pick something filthy out of the manure. She looked at it, brushed it off a little. The girls watching her shrieked and groaned and made make-sick sounds. Annakey stood up and walked away.

She walked to the end of the village. People laughed as she went by, thinking it had been an accident. She did not notice, for her mind was fast upon the thing she had found in the chicken offal. She walked past Oda Weedbridge's house. She walked to the end of the valley to where the mountains begin to bunch up their toes, and into the pathless forest. She walked until she reached the place where the river comes down from the mountain, until she came to her secret place.

When she was there she washed the thing she had found in the manure and put it into her sheep's meadow.

It was the same little man she had swept up in my house years ago, the one I had thrown into the yard. She studied the man doll, and studied it more, until she knew.

How many times had Annakey desired to fill her meadow with sheep or cows or goats, and then remembered that she must not disobey me. Now she would not keep her promise, for she knew the man doll was her father, and she would make a valley for him and a story for herself.

ANNAKEY BATHED in the cold river until she was clean. For a long time she sat by the river in the sun, until the pain in her chest eased. She touched her promise doll on the thong around her neck and stared at the little man doll standing beside her sheep. Comparing the two, she could see that the sheep was the work of a child, accurate, but withholding something. She took more clay from the river. She made another sheep.

This time she felt different. As her hand caressed the slippery clay, she felt a wisdom in her eye, a love in her fingers, a cunning in her wrists and thumbs. This time she thought less about accurate imitation. Now she thought about a sheep, how it was to be a sheep, to know all the little grasses blade by blade, and to be able to pick them one at a time with your teeth. She knew the smell of field and wood, earth and leaf. She was a sheep, smelling the earth, tasting it. She felt her dainty hoof treading among the gilly mushrooms, the tickle of a ladybug in her ear, and the pain of hoofrot. She knew the taste of bluebells, saw the dew that gathered in the dimples of the earth—wine, sweet wine. She felt the warm, musky comfort of her fellows all round, ever-round day and night, safe, safe.

Then she felt a desire to walk away to that dandelion, or that clover. She knew that she was fashioning Follownot, Oda's sheep, who was fed in winter on chopped straw and dried peas, and who had such a taste for flowers she would wander away from the herd.

She did not know she was feeling power. She could only feel her joy that when she was done it was a fine thing, and that she could see into the little thing's eyes and know its name. "Follownot," she said. She had begun to make a valley doll, and she knew how.

WHEN ANNAKEY PUT THE MAN DOLL in the little meadow, she began to make her own story. You must understand this if you are to understand how it happened that the next day Manal and Areth brought to my house black feathers that they had found. Within hours the whole village knew that the robber people had found our valley. There was weeping and wailing while everyone searched their houses and fields to see if the robber people had stolen anything. The only thing that came up missing was Oda Weedbridge's sheep, Follownot.

[Chapter 7]

INSCRIPTION ON THE RECIPE DOLL:
Rutabagas: Oil the greens, toss with salt.
Boil the root with butter and bones. Mash
the meat or bake into bread. Give the peel-
ings to the pig.

ANNAKEY WAS HARD at cleaning my chicken coop the next morning when Areth and Manal came to me with the black feathers.

"This is not possible," I said to Manal when he reported that Oda's sheep Follownot was missing.

"It is true," Oda said. She had come with the boys.

"In my hidden village doll, there is a sheep named Follownot," I said to Oda. "He is hidden there still, beneath a sky blanket, behind closed doors. The robber people could not have found him here in the valley. You let him wander out of the safety of the valley onto the mountain where he was eaten by a cat."

Manal cleared his throat. "Dollmage," he said, "he was taken out of the sheepcote. That is where we found the feather they left for Follownot."

I ran to check the village doll in my secret room. Had mice eaten holes in the blanket? No. How could I have known that the village story was being taken away from me?

When I returned, Oda was speaking harshly to Annakey while she kept to her work. "You have brought bad luck to my house. It is that frowning promise doll you wear. You killed your own mother with it, and now you will kill me. Already it has begun, for my sheep is stolen."

Before you know what Annakey answered, you must know this: Annakey Rainsayer loved three things and feared only one thing. This makes her unusual from the beginning, for most of us love one thing—ourselves—and fear many things. Because we fear more things than we love, our lives are blown this way and that way by our fears.

I have already told you one thing Annakey loved: doll-making. It was her first joy. The first joys last forever.

Now, in her concern for her people, Annakey discovered a new love. She loved her valley. She loved the crooked creek that wound through, changing its mind and twisting a different direction every league, and the little brick footbridges that arced over the creek at every twist and turn. She loved the mountains that made it a valley. She loved Mount Lair for its woods and waterfalls, and the stags among the firs, forgetting that it was unfriendly to men, that in its everchanging undergrowth men had been lost to death.

Who can account for the way Annakey thought? The mountains are dangerous, wild with forests that are filled with bears and wolves and cougar cats. Their brows are menacing, their snows impassable in winter. But Annakey saw that they offered their green feet for gardens, their meadows for summer grazing, their high pines for firewood, and their dark forests for game. Their rivers filled the valley with cold white water and fish in the water. The mountains frowned down the clouds and took the brunt of the cold winds so that the snow in Seekvalley fell gently and straight down.

Mostly the reason Annakey loved the valley was because in it was her people. Why did she—does she—love you? Perhaps, you think, it is because you cared for your yards, decorating them with rockeries and flowerbeds, ponds and trellis-es. Perhaps she loved you because you built little bridges, and gave them names like Coffee-At-My-House, and Come-Sit-By-My-Fire, and Visit More. Perhaps it was because she loved to see the mothers in their kitchens, wielding their rolling pins, making biscuits and pies and loaves, rubbing their knuckles off onto washerboards, then tending their babies gently with their worn, rough hands. Perhaps she loves you because you are a fair folk, tall and curly-haired and green-eyed. Surely she loves you for your songs and fine poetry.

It was none of these things that made her love you, her people, though she loved all these things. No. What was most precious to Annakey was that her people kept their promises. This, she recognized, was their worship. What they spoke became what was. Bagger Cornfield once promised Annakey the best melon from his garden. When harvest time came, Bagger, who was never the smartest one in the village, real-ized he could not tell which melon was the best. Though Annakey released him from his promise, he would not be released. He cut every ripe melon in two to see which was the pinkest and the sweetest and the most succulent. Of course the melons had to be eaten right away, so he held a melon party for the village. You remember? For a little while he regretted his promise, all his lovely melons eaten. But after the party—is it not true?—everyone loved him a little better than before. It is always best to keep one's promises.

Annakey loved the way the old women cared for their old husbands long after they had stopped being of any use to them—because they had promised. She loved you for the way you raised your children and fed them, even when they were ugly babies, which seldom happens, and even when they became ugly adolescents, which often happens. This is why Annakey loved her people, and why, when she heard the robber people had taken Follownot, she was sick with fear and shame. She knew now the power in her hands, and she knew she was responsible.

Some of you nod your heads now and stroke the stones at your sides. You are right to stone her, you say. You do not care that she loved you, her people, that even now she loves you enough not to hate you for binding her, for dragging her to be executed. Look, look into her eyes. Yes, that is good. Look, and see, and remember.

Now I have told you two things that Annakey loved. The third I shall tell you shortly. The children say, "The story, the story." They are right. What matters but the story? I continue.

"Leave her be, Oda," Manal said when Oda accused Annakey. "It is not her fault."

"Perhaps it is, Manal," Annakey said softly. She propped the shovel and came closer. "I made a sheep. Yesterday. I called him Follownot."

I looked at her long in silence. The skin at her throat was quivering and goose-fleshed. I said, "Bring me this sheep."

Annakey began to walk away. Manal went with her. He followed her silently, without thinking, and she accepted his presence silently, without thought. As they walked I knew a thing.

I knew the third thing Annakey loved was Manal.

How can I tell you the strength of their love? Would my silence tell the matter more? How strange are words to both give and take away meaning. But you see him at her side now, willing to share her fate. That will tell you more than words will.

Annakey and Manal had befriended each other as only children can since they had herded the sheep together. But now Manal had come to love Annakey as a man loves a woman. I will tell you how.

Manal had been hunting the day Annakey ran to her secret place to bathe away the chicken manure from her body. The hunt had been unsuccessful. He decided to return home by the river way, tired of climbing over rotting timber and slogging through scummed pools in the bog forest. Just as Annakey emerged naked from the water, her hair gleaming wet and long down her back, her skin shining in the sun, Manal came to the bank on the opposite side of the river and saw what he thought was a wood nymph. A moment later he knew it was not a wood nymph, but that it was Annakey. Manal had thought Annakey the gentlest soul of all the village girls, and fair of face as well. He had cherished her as his childhood friend and was on her side whenever there was a side to be on. Now he saw her new, a wild thing, like the forest animals, and beautiful as the river. Though as a boy he had always cared for her, now as a man he desired her.

A lesser man might have taken advantage of Annakey then, far away as she was from the village. He might even have waited and watched as long as he could, or he might have come and spoken to her. But Manal was a fine hunter, wise in the knowledge that every footprint left in the virgin forest takes a winter to vanish, and that a misfired arrow will chase away the animals for an entire season. No, instead Manal walked in the woods along the riverbank until he was far from Annakey. Then he took his big boots and stomped through the cold, rushy river until his groin stopped tormenting him and the cold water made his fingernails blue and the cold sweat ran out of his long, dark hair. The next morning he was up at dawn, still thinking of Annakey, and that is when he heard Oda crying for her sheep.

How Manal glares. He does not want his story told. And yet, Manal, I must. It is no longer in my hands. If Annakey is executed, I know you will lose your life trying to defend her. Your story must be told, just in case.

This much all of you know: Manal was the best boy of the village. He was not the best at everything, but he was the one all the other boys measured themselves by. Atur Longbody was the best runner in the village because he was the only one who could sometimes outrun Manal. Areth was the best cattleman in the valley, because his were the only cows that were fatter than Manal's. Kello Naplong grew the juiciest corn and Wagon Dogkeep the hardiest wheat because theirs was better than Manal's. Manal was the second best at everything in fact, except hunting. For that Manal has been named Masterhunter.

As I had promised, he grew to be very like Mount Crownantler. He was the tallest boy in the village, just as Crownantler was the tallest of the mountains. He was a silent man, like the mountain. The mountain peak bore ice even in the summer, and so also did Manal keep his emotions cool even in anger. Crownantler was not friendly to the valley people, and no one but Renoa could climb it far. So also Manal kept a distance from most people.

But he promised his heart to Annakey.

It shows the depth of her trust that she took Manal to her secret place after I had sent her to fetch the sheep she had made. Manal never betrayed her trust. He was silent as she led him to her bower. He did not tell her he had the previous day seen this bower from the other side of the river.

"And here, in the hole of this tree, I have a blanket, and fishing wire and flint and dried fruit. I shall run away and stay here," Annakey said. "I will make a story for my father."

"Annakey, did you make this?"

Manal was standing over the valley doll that Annakey had begun on the large, flat rock by the river.

She nodded. "It is not quite right. It is not like our valley."

Manal turned to her. Now, in addition to his affection and desire, Manal loved her. He looked at her in wonder and admiration. "Now I know you are the Dollmage," he said quietly. "You cannot run away. Our people need you."

"It is what I have desired, Manal," she said. "I cannot help seeing the story of the village with my hands."

He turned back to the doll. "You must build the doll of a house. Make it a fine house."

"A house?"

"Yes."

"Whose?"

"Mine. Ours, if you will."

Annakey bent and picked up the sheep Follownot. "Ours? You will do as Areth and ask me to promise to marry you?"

"No. I make a promise of myself. One day you may return my love, but if not, it will not change my promise to you that I will love only you."

The best loves begin this way. The longest loves last this way.

No, I will not tell you what she answered. Have you no dignity? Will you give them no privacy?

Suffice it to say they returned to me.

She held the sheep in her hand, loose at her side, relaxed. She did not bow her head.

"Show it to me," I said. Renoa leaned over my shoulder to look, too.

Annakey showed me the sheep. She hoped I would see

the power in her hands. I did. It was more than a replica. It had the field in it, and when I looked in its eyes, I saw. I saw.

Renoa grabbed the clay sheep from Annakey's hand. "This sheep is not like Follownot. Where is his ribbon?"

"It is like, but for that," I said, my voice trembling. I did not think to ask Annakey if she had made anything else.

Renoa picked up a bit of thin ribbon and tied it around the clay sheep's neck. "There. Oda Weedbridge always placed a ribbon around her sheep's neck, like this."

She smiled up at me, hoping for my approval, but saw only pity in my countenance.

"Yes," Annakey said. "That is better, Renoa." In her voice I could hear the confidence a Dollmage has in her art, and pity for Renoa. Renoa heard it, too.

She looked from me to Manal to Annakey. Then, before I could stop her, Renoa threw the clay sheep into the fire and ran out of the house.

I let her go.

"Did you not promise me that you would make no more animal dolls? To break a promise is punishable by death. I will counsel the villagers to be lenient, but one who has broken a promise can never be Dollmage."

Annakey stood tall. Something inside her had changed, and I had not seen it. Or perhaps I changed, for until that moment I had interpreted her gentleness and cheer for weakness, not knowing the strength it took to choose it. Now I saw her strength.

"Release me from my promise, Dollmage, since I made the sheep for a companion to my father's doll that I found in your chicken coop."

So.

That was it. She knew my terrible secret, and what I had done to her father and to Vilsa and to herself.

So.

"I release you," I said. I turned away from her and slammed the door.

That night I wept in my pillow for it. I prayed to God and asked him why he gave me to put a frown on her promise doll and then gave her the gift to make this sheep. He answered me in a puzzling way (so like Him): He told me the one thing that Annakey feared.

Now I will tell you.

Annakey was afraid of the power that she knew was in her hands.

Do not pretend you do not know of what I speak. Do we not all fear the power that is in us to do good, to love, to make the world better? It is not our dark souls that frighten us. We are familiar with that part of ourselves. It is the glory parts, the singing, ploughing, dreaming, loving parts that terrify us.

Annakey Rainsayer, deep in her heart where she would not look, was afraid that she was powerful indeed. It was her light that frightened her, her ability to make unspeakable beauty in the world. As a young girl she had thought to win love, to make others better by making herself small. She had thought to find peace by making herself invisible. Foolish girl. Not that she was entirely wrong, for one can win a certain peace by being small and invisible. But Annakey could not be Dollmage because she was afraid.

It comforted my heart to know that Annakey was afraid of something, and I said thank you to God. He seemed cold to me, as if I had not gotten the point.

The next day I told her what God had told me about her.

I thought to punish her for humiliating me, and almost I thought it had worked. She nodded and said, "Yes, Dollmage. You are right."

How was I to know that she would learn from my rebuke? It is so rare. I did not anticipate.

"THE STORY! THE STORY!" the children complain. The children speak, but even the adults tire of my wisdom and wish me only to get on with the story. You are helpless before it. Poor. Poor. I weep for you, for soon we come to the part of the story that will drag down your heart.

Men were set to watch the village at night, and in the day they searched for the robber people in the lower parts of the mountain. So it was that Manal Masterhunter found the remains of Oda's sheep Follownot. He found her bones and the ribbon she had been wearing, all beside a fire built and left by the robber people. Follownot had been cooked.

Soon after I heard the news, I found Renoa hiding in her mother's root shed.

"Come, Dollmage Renoa," I said. "You threw the sheep into the fire and now it is cooked. Your naming ceremony will be at the next full moon. Prepare yourself."

[Chapter 8]

INSCRIPTION ON THE WAR DOLL:
*Thabana Firstpeople had a son who nursed
hard upon her, making her nipples bleed.*

*"What is blood," she said, "so long as
my child has milk?"*

I SEE YOU TIRE OF THIS NEVER KNOWING.

Try to think of me for a change.

You, Greppa Lowmeadow, chafe at the length of my story. Your execution feast is eaten. Give us those baked eggs then.

RENOA WORKED HARD THE NEXT DAY. When I wanted to rest, she said, "No, Dollmage, teach me more. Teach me everything." Her hands were strong and wise. I announced Renoa's naming day. The people relaxed a little, confident that the new, young Dollmage would find a way to rid us of the robber people.

That night, three sheep were stolen. Also two saws, a trowel, a ladder, five pitchforks, and a pig.

I took Renoa to the back room where the village doll lay under the sky blanket.

"Why is the sky blanket no longer protecting us?" I asked her.

"You ask me?" Renoa sneered.

I gripped the edge of the table and leaned over it.

"Hide us," I said.

Fear stopped up Renoa's mouth as she realized she had not

the power to save herself. How could she have known that the story of the village was being made in another place, in broad daylight, and by other hands?

You villagers, in your anxiety and distress, could hardly eat that day, never mind attend to your labors. I do not criticize. It was understandable. A crowd of you came to my door.

"Why do you not protect us, Dollmage?" the fieldmaster asked. There were supportive murmurs throughout the crowd. "The robber people make our lives hard, and one day it will be impossible to stay in our valley. What are you doing about it? Will you let our crops be carried off? Soon it will be women and children."

"How dare you question me!" I retorted. Bil Brokehoe cowered a little before me, which made me benevolent.

"Forgive us, Dollmage Hobblefoot," said Norda Banter-cross. "We are afraid."

Everyone fell silent, then. To speak it aloud made it more real. I punished you with your fear for a time, and refused to comfort you. Then, I said, "Renoa will be named the new Dollmage at the next full moon."

In your fear of the robber people, you had forgotten your uneasiness with Annakey. Furthermore, Manal, who everyone respected, had been talking.

"Dollmage," said Norda, "we have talked among ourselves and discussed this over the common fire. Annakey has shown her gift, and so has Renoa. Who should be Dollmage? The one who made the sheep that was cooked? Or the one who threw it in the fire? The one who made the cow who was drowned, or the one who threw it in the water? The one who made the sky blanket that hid the village doll, or the one who put it over the village doll?"

In my rage I could not speak. Norda cleared her throat.

"Could it be that God knew in advance of our trouble, that he knew it would be trouble enough for two?"

"Two is divisive," I said. "There can only be one in a village. The law is clear."

Annakey spoke from the edge of the crowd. "Do not fear," she said gently. Her voice was soft, but everyone heard. "We will save you from the robber people. I promise."

Making such a promise was as absurd as promising her mother that she would be happy. Now Annakey had made two promises in her life. That is two too many. But the people were calmed by her words, as if there were a power in them.

"She can make no such promise," I said.

"She is not the Dollmage," Renoa said.

Renoa and I were not willing to stake our reputations and what we took as our good graces with God by risking such a rash promise.

"So, if Renoa is the Dollmage, then we are doomed?" someone called. There came murmurs, then a woman began to freely weep, and her baby to wail. Another woman fainted.

Renoa said sharply, "I will do what I can to protect you, of course, but we are in God's hands."

"A contest," someone said, and I saw that it was Manal.

"A contest, a contest," took up the crowd.

I saw that they would not settle. "I will do as you say," I said above the clamor. When they had quieted somewhat, I said, "There will be a contest to which all of you may be witness. Whoever of the two girls can make the best doll, a doll with power in itself, that girl you must support unquestioningly as the new Dollmage. The other will have to swear and promise before the entire village that she will not use her powers again forever, or be banished alone to the mountains. It will be decided at the full moon."

At this the crowd began to disperse. When they were all gone, Renoa stood before Annakey and slapped her face. Annakey did not back away.

"You had no right," Renoa said fiercely to her. "How could you promise to save them? Only the Dollmage can save them, and that is me."

I said, "You have brought embarrassment upon yourself, Annakey."

"I have obeyed your counsel, Dollmage," she said. "I will no longer be afraid of what is in me. The story of the village will have a happy ending. I have decided."

I watched her in silence as the welts rose on her cheek. I took a secret comfort in the promise she had made to save the village. I did not hear her practically confess that she had stolen the story of the village from my hands.

"Go away from me," I said.

She did not move. "I must learn what I can from you."

I took a deep breath. "Well," I said, "now there must be a contest. Renoa, you may begin now to make your contest doll. Annakey, for your presumption, I have work for you to do. It will keep you too busy to attend the village dance tonight."

RIBB WIFEBURY had wanted to build a potting shed in his garden. I made it, and placed it in the village doll, in the center of the Wifebury garden, beside the sundial in the middle of the long daisies. I set Annakey to cleaning up the mess I had made in my creation, and to add Ribb's muddy boots beside the chopping block. I went about my business. When I returned in the evening, she had cleaned up the mess, as well as dug up a bucket of rutabagas for breakfast. I hid my pleasure and surprise, until I saw what she had done with the potting shed.

Besides the boots, she had made for the potting shed doll

a miniature coil of rope, a broom, an ax, a workbench, and a bag of seeds. There were tiny seedlings on the workbench, and for the garden, most marvelous of all, bees. Almost invisible they were. Tiny bees in the garden—they would make the Wifebury garden the most luscious in the valley. How had she learned to do such beautiful work?

I did not know that she had also found time to make the doll of a house for Manal, a warm house for winter, a cool house for summer, a sound house to last the life of a man.

"It is marvelous," I said, touching the tiny seedlings that lined the window of the potting shed.

"Thank you, Dollmage," Annakey said. She was glowing with joy to be free finally to do dollwork.

I looked at her long, then. Could it be that she was winning my heart? How different they were: my Renoa, who tamed deer and fed hawks from her hand and knew the mountain as well as the valley; and Annakey, who loved hearth and home and all the art of it.

The miniatures she made worked their magic on me, and I said, "Annakey, you have done enough today. You may go to the dance."

Annakey smiled. "Thank you, Dollmage." She went to the cupboard and took out of it a lovely little cake, decorated with icing flowers. "I made this for Renoa, so that we might be friends. I will give it to her at the dance."

"Why do you do this? Renoa struck you," I said.

"If I were to make the village story, it would be with all of us at peace together," she said firmly.

I was too concerned about the robber people and too enchanted by potting shed bees to be overly annoyed that the frowning doll I had made for her was not working still. I listened at my window to the music and the laughter.

The dance was a ploy. Our people are born into the promise that we will not kill, unless it is to defend our children.
Since the robber people had not taken a child, we could not
defend ourselves from them in that way. Still, we were not
born into a promise to be afraid. Fieldmaster Sodder had
declared that there would be a dance that night so that the
robber people would see that we were not afraid.

Even though we were.

The common fire lighted the village and the music filled
the valley as Annakey approached the dancers. The ones who
had loved her as boys now loved her as men. Miller touched
her arm and spoke to her, smiling. Tawm Herson twirled her
gently and asked her to dance. Miller watched her with
resigned eyes as she made her way over to Renoa. He knew
she would never love him.

Is it not so, Miller? Is that why, in spite of your love, you
have a stone in your hand? If you cannot have her, you would
that no one has her. In thinking this way, you have broken
every promise you were born into. Put down your stone. You,
at least, will take no part in Annakey's execution if I am
unable to persuade the rest.

Annakey gave Renoa the cake she had made for her, smiling and saying something kind.

Renoa did not smile, and because she did not, neither did
her friends. Renoa's storymaker was so powerful that others
submitted to it and allowed themselves to be mere characters
in her world. Once they were in her story, it was difficult to
escape, for if they did they might disappear.

Of course Manal was there at the dance, waiting for
Annakey. He saw her take the cake to Renoa and offer it to
her. Annakey's hair was disheveled from her work, but it
framed her face even more beautifully. Her frock was thin

from wear and a little too short, but that only allowed him to imagine more fully the narrow hips beneath.

Now, you must understand. To be loved by Manal was not a small thing. He had a self-promise of which he was deeply aware and which he honored above all other promises. Manal had promised himself that he would have a great love. This self-promise was Manal's only flaw in an otherwise perfect man, a man of spare promises. The promise to love is the biggest and most generous and most terrifying promise of all, and we all know what trouble it can cause.

And so, when Manal fell in love with Annakey, it was like an earthquake. Though it appeared as only a quiver on his lips, a momentary rocking on his feet, it changed everything. Like an earthquake, it made waterfalls where none before had been, hills to rise and valleys to fall. Poor Manal. You see why he cannot help that he must try to stop as many of you as he can if you stone his Annakey. You see why he must die trying to defend her. That night, however, he wanted only to spend his life with her.

"I knew Dollmage would let you come," Manal said. "She is not evil, only afraid." He said it, not I.

Annakey shook her head and laughed. "I cannot recall ever seeing Dollmage afraid of anything."

Manal laughed. "Nor I, but one. She is afraid of your frowning promise doll."

"Everyone is afraid of it," Annakey said. "Even my mother was."

"I am not."

"Not?"

"I understand what it means."

"Tell me."

Manal shook his head and smiled. "I will. For a kiss."

Annakey said nothing for a long time. She looked thoughtful. Finally, she said, "My mother taught me that a kiss was a kind of promise, and that great care must be taken with such promises. So . . . no."

Manal laughed, and then he stopped laughing, for everything she said and did made him love her more.

"I made you a house," Annakey said.

"I will come and see it tomorrow."

"Do you remember this dance?" she said, taking his hand and laughing. "The Lady-Under? We learned it as children."

"My head forgets, but perhaps my feet will remember." They joined into the dance. Their bodies understood each other. I could see that, as they danced the jigs and reels. Star, square, circle, promenade: They moved in rhythm to the music and to each other. They danced as if they had been dancing every day of their lives.

I have told you that Manal was the best boy in the village, and so of course who should set her sights upon him other than my Renoa. She loved the way he knew the forest paths as well as she, and respected him for his understanding of the wild beasts. She flirted with Manal, and he had responded to her in the pure delight a man takes in any woman. Since he had fallen in love with Annakey, however, he had been distant with Renoa. She did not know why. She only knew it made her desire him more. Now, when Renoa saw Annakey and Manal together at the dance, she saw that while she herself was any woman, Annakey was the woman.

That night, Manal and Annakey danced together every dance. They laughed and talked at the surface of things and at the bottom of things. Though Manal had been Annakey's special friend since childhood, Annakey of late had begun to look at him with the yearning eyes of one who looks upon her treasure. As she danced, she touched his shoulders and arms as one who outlines her world with her hands.

I told you that Renoa had her eye upon Manal. Now I will tell you that Areth had his eye upon Annakey. He did not love her, as Manal did, because of the art of her hands, or, as Manal did, because she always smiled even with a frowning promise doll. He did not love her, as Manal did, because of the way she breathed and moved and dreamed. Areth loved her because she was beautiful, but more than that Areth loved her because Manal loved her. Also, because he thought she was easy to boss.

My Renoa was not entirely spoiled. When she saw that Manal wanted Annakey, she turned her attentions to Areth. When she saw that Areth wanted Annakey too, she became filled with hate. How can I blame her? Annakey was stealing everything that made Renoa smile. Renoa told herself that Annakey was draining the smiles from her promise doll as she had with her own mother.

Why is it that everything that was bad in her life made Renoa miserable, whereas when bad things happened to Annakey, she remained happy? Annakey had promised herself she would be happy. What had Renoa promised herself? That she would have what she wanted. There is the difference. Of course, that may be the moral of the story, but I will not punish you by explaining it. The bad egg and the gristly stew and the woody potatoes all together do not add up to such abuse. As I told you, I am selfish and weak, not evil.

The dance music became louder and wilder and the common fire burned hotter and brighter. Steal from us what you will, the dancers seemed to say to any robber people that might be watching, you cannot steal from us this night our joy in being alive, and in our bodies that can do this and this and this.

Annakey and Manal became separated in the dancing. Annakey saw Manal dancing with Renoa, and then Areth was with her. While they danced, Areth placed his hands on Annakey's body where they should not be. The elders were all too riotous to notice.

"I am a man, now, Annakey," Areth said into her ear. "Do not stop me."

"If you are a man, stop yourself," Annakey said, moving away.

Areth was surprised. He had thought Annakey was easy to boss. Of course, Annakey was the hardest to boss. She was the only one I could not boss, though many a night I wept in my pillow for it. Annakey would not allow her promise to her mother to go unfulfilled. She would be happy, and that was that.

Areth found himself looking into the face of Manal. As I have said, Manal was like Mount Crownantler, full of weather. The weather at that moment was a black storm. Areth too was like a mountain, and though it was the smaller Southslope Mountain, still he was high and proud. He met Manal's glare. At that moment Renoa began weeping loudly, and all her friends gathered around to comfort her.

"What is it?" they asked, but Renoa appeared unable to be consoled.

"What is it?" a few of the elders nearby asked.

Annakey went to Renoa. "What is it?" she asked.

"You!" Renoa said to her, in the hearing of all around them. "It is you. How could you play such a trick on me?"

"I? What?" Annakey asked.

Renoa held up the pretty cake that Annakey had made her. "Yes, you. You gave me this cake thinking to apologize for the hurts you have caused me, but when I went to bite into it, I smelled this." Renoa held the cake up to Annakey's nose, and Annakey recoiled from the strong scent of chicken manure. Renoa held up the cake to her other friends, who each exclaimed in turn at the stench of the cake.

"You rolled the cake in chicken manure," one of the friends said to Annakey.

"No," Annakey said. "I didn't. I wouldn't."

"She would not do that," Manal said. "Perhaps Renoa dropped the cake and in the dark did not notice into what it had fallen."

"I did not drop the cake," Renoa said sharply, and then she began to weep again, and fell on Manal's chest. Manal stepped away from her as if she had the pox. Renoa's tears stopped as suddenly as they had begun. Annakey had seen that expression before. Renoa was angry, and Annakey knew she would be the brunt of that anger. Renoa was angrier than she had ever been before.

"Shameful," said one of the elders who had been listening. It was Oda Weedbridge.

"A disgusting prank," said one of Oda's cronies.

Soon, many of the elders were comforting Renoa and casting accusing glances at Annakey. This was when Annakey began to grow in wisdom. All her life growing up, she thought the villagers knew her and loved her as she knew and loved them. At that moment she realized they did not know her at all, for if they did they could not believe such a thing of her. She clutched her promise doll and tried to remember that the things she loved about her people had not changed.

"Renoa, you are lying," Manal said.

"Manal, you are defending her because you fear that if you do not, she will choose Areth over yourself," Oda Weedbridge said.

"I have no such fear," Manal said.

At this Areth stepped forward. "Why is that? Because you think you are better than me?" Now Manal truly was better, and that had been griping at Areth since they were boys. He threw a punch at Manal, surprising everyone. Why were you surprised? It had been coming for a long time. Of course Manal punched back. Now both boys were well liked in the village, and so you might imagine that not a few of the others joined the brawl. Soon the elders of the village had to be called away from their posts at watch to stop the fight.

I went to fetch the girls.

FOR A LONG TIME I treated them to my silence. I made them sit far from the fire, and then I told them they had spoiled the dance and who knew what trouble would come of that. Would the robber people see that we were weak because we were not united? I refused to listen to either one of them. I doubted Annakey had played the trick on Renoa, but I loved my Renoa, and the smell of wild herbs in her hair. I suspected Renoa had lied, but I also understood her tempers. Finally I spoke.

"This comes because of the contest. Even thinking there may be two Dollmages has divided us. It is obvious that you two girls cannot live in the same village as equals," I said to them. "For now, I have a plan. The elders of the village are worried about those who took the herds to the summer meadows up on the mountain. They fear the robber people will find them and steal our sheep all away. They have asked me to build a doll of the sheepcote and the summer meadow and hide it. It has been too many years since I have been to the summer meadow and I do not remember it well enough to make a doll of it. I am too old to make the climb now. You will go in my place, Annakey."

"No, send me, Grandmother Hobblefoot," Renoa said. "It is my place, in the mountain."

"No, Renoa, you will stay and work on your contest doll." I knew she wanted to go, but at long last I would discipline her.

"Thank you for trusting me with this task, Dollmage," Annakey said. "I will prove to you that I can be Dollmage." Then she stopped and said, "If I am in the summer meadow, when will I have time to make my contest doll?"

"When you get back there will be time enough. The true Dollmage will find a way to do what she must."

Annakey frowned a little. That softened me. "It is a long climb to the summer meadow," I said, "and there are bears. You may take a companion with you, a friend."

I felt regret as I watched Annakey struggle to think who might be her friend. I realized that a few of the girls knew Annakey enough to like her, but they were afraid to defend her. Anyone who befriended Annakey was sure to bring the same torment from Renoa upon herself. I determined to speak to Renoa about her behavior and looked at her sternly as I thought it.

"I will ask Manal," Annnakey said finally.

"No!" Renoa said. She looked up at my disapproving face and said, "Do not let her. It—it is not appropriate."

"Why? If they start early in the morning, they can be at the summer meadow before nightfall." It annoyed me that Renoa should be jealous over anyone but myself. "Now apologize to Annakey. You must learn to be her friend, to overcome personal feelings, if you are to be a good Dollmage."

Renoa's face calmed immediately. It went very white. Then she smiled.

"I am sorry, Annakey," she said, only she looked at me when she said it.

"To prove your friendship," I said to Renoa, "go tell Manal yourself that Annakey has chosen him to accompany her to the summer meadow."

Renoa ran. She was gone a long time.

By the time she returned, Annakey had packed the things she would need for her journey.

"Manal said to start without him. He must first do the chores, but he will catch up to you before the morning is half over."

Annakey smiled. She need not have, for Renoa had not told Manal. She told Areth, who now both loved and hated Annakey.

[Chapter 9]

INSCRIPTION ON THE JUSTICE DOLL:
*Wherever possible the people will try to
blame the victim.*

AH. IT IS DIFFICULT FOR ME TO GO ON. My neck aches with
the heaviness of my memories, with the horror of what happened next. That is what comes with a lifetime of sin and stu-
pidity. What should I expect? Part of my neck-ache comes
from the gristly stew and the bad egg, Greppa.

This is the part of the story when Annakey truly becomes
wise. How we all wish for wisdom, and yet there is a price to
pay for it. After wisdom comes, gone is the joy that fills each
morning upon waking, simply because it is another day. That
inexplicable, unblamable joy—it makes my back arch with
pleasure just to remember it. But it is only a memory, for now
I, too, am wise.

I will give you an example.

A child there was once, in the days of my grandmother,
who was a careful child. She was obedient and manageable,
and all the old folks thought her to be much like themselves
when they were young: perfect. She liked always to be clean,
and to play in a sedate and cautious manner. She took no
risks, tried nothing new, and never failed. Needless to say,
nothing bad ever happened to her. She took to hanging a little hood over her promise doll so that it remained as

unmarked by soil or sun as it had been in the beginning. We all know that as the wood ages it discolors, cracks, and peels, never in the same way as another. That explains how we get wrinkles and age spots. Now, this girl never aged. Her skin stayed as smooth and bland as a child's. Many men courted her, but none wanted to marry her. She was good to look at, but boring. She was never wise. She stayed with her mother all her life and was a burden to her in her old age.

A sad story.

I am full of them.

The next morning, Annakey left early, her pack full with the things she would need for a journey to the summer meadow up on the mountain. She had packed extra flatbread and fruit leather for Manal, who Renoa had again assured her would meet her on the trail by midmorning.

Annakey was happy. The day was bright on the mountains, the shadows small and cherry black beneath the pine. Birdsong echoed in the wood, and in Annakey's heart. She was not afraid of the bears. They are late sleepers. She had hiked far by midmorning, passing the woodcutter's cabin and the rotting bee tree, when she heard Manal's footsteps coming up the path behind her. She stopped and waited for him.

It was not Manal. It was Areth.

Annakey could not hide the disappointment in her face for a moment. She had learned, however, that there was more happiness in being kind to others than in having what you want. So she smiled.

That was the last time Annakey smiled, for a long time. Finally, her frowning promise doll would have its way.

"It is me and not Manal," Areth said. He was not smiling.

"So I see. Is Manal coming behind?"

"No."

"Come then. We will climb a while, and then we will eat. I brought extra for—for you."

"No. We will rest now," Areth said.

"Come," Annakey said, gesturing to him. She was already walking.

"Now, I said."

There was danger in his voice. Annakey stopped. If she had known just how much danger, she would have run.

Slowly, she took the food from her pack. Areth was sweating and breathing hard. He did not look at the food, but at Annakey.

"What is troubling you, Areth?" Annakey said at last.

"You know."

Areth was one of those people who always assumed that when hurt came to him the other person had done it purposely.

"I do not know," Annakey said. "But we are friends, and so you can tell me."

"Why did you lead me to believe that you loved me, when all along you loved Manal?" Areth said.

He was not really asking, and deep in his heart he knew that she had led him to believe no such thing. He was merely justifying in his own ears what he knew he was going to do.

"I have promised myself to no one," Annakey said. She put down the buttered bread. She felt as if there were a worm in her stomach.

"You smiled at me, and you were kind to me, and praised my husbandry."

"Everyone praises your husbandry, Areth. You are the best in the village, even better than Manal."

Areth spat. "I am tired of everyone comparing themselves to Manal, as if to be better than him is a true feat."

Annakey took a bite of her bread as if everything was all right, as if the air was not singing with danger. She chewed and chewed, but the bread would not go down.

"There are unspoken promises," Areth said. "The way you treated me was an unspoken promise that you would be mine."

"I am your friend, Areth," Annakey said. "I have always been your friend—"

Areth slapped her mouth shut.

"We will be more than friends, you and I," he said hoarsely. He pulled her near him and clutched at her breast. Annakey pulled away so violently she freed herself.

"How dare you treat a virgin of the village so," Annakey said, panting with fear and fury.

"No virgin," Areth said. "Last night I slept in the field with the other men on guard. In his sleep, I heard Manal speak about your breasts as a man who had seen them."

Annakey shook her head. "No. Manal has always treated me with respect."

"What you gave to Manal, you will give to me," Areth said.

She was standing now. Only a little while ago, the forest on either side of the path had been dark and full of cougar and wolf. Now it seemed welcome, a place full of only childish nightmares. On the path she could not outrun Areth, but perhaps in the forest. Annakey ran.

She could not outrun Areth.

When he caught up to her, he pushed her hard and then was on top of her before she could get her breath.

"You have promised me with your eyes and your smile and your gentle ways," Areth said. With one hand he covered her mouth and with the other he pulled up her dress and looked at her breasts. Annakey bit his hand and he pulled it away with a yelp. That gave him reason to do what he was going to do anyway.

"Areth!" she cried. "Do not force me." Annakey began to weep. "I will promise you anything. . . ."

Areth could not remember having seen her cry before. He stopped, there on top of her, crushing her. He looked around himself as if waking up from a dream. He pushed himself up on one arm. "Promise me you will marry me," he said.

Annakey's mouth moved but she did not speak.

"Promise me you will marry me," he said angrily. His hand closed around her neck as he said it.

"I promise," she said. The agony in her voice rang through the forest.

Areth looked at her. Now that she was his, she was not so beautiful in his eyes anymore. Now that she was his, she was no more to him than one of his fine cows that he cared for— not because he loved them, but because then he would be the best in the village. Now that she was his, he despised her.

And because he despised her, he forced her anyway.

ANNAKEY DID NOT SCREAM. Horrors come in silence.

"I'm sorry," he said, when he was done. He began to cry, and then he stopped, angry that she did not sympathize with his pain.

Annakey stood, shaking, and without looking back, began to climb the hill.

YOU LOOK AT ME AND LOOK AT ME, expecting me to go on. Ah. What has gone out of me? Why can I not make words for what Annakey felt? Is it because I am old? Have I traded every passion for wisdom, every love for tolerance, every wild and wicked dream for a full stomach and a soft bed? When did I know that there was nothing to know? All the sharpness and selfishness and wild laughter is gone, and I am never in one moment. Now when I laugh, I see a child who died. When I weep, I know that weeping will cease and I will laugh again. Well. There will be no more first tastes, but also gone are the fears that lived in all my dark places. Now, all the dark places have been plunged into, and I cannot see where the light ends and the dark begins. I am fearless and speechless. I cannot mourn out your mourning for Annakey with words. You must find them in your own heart, in your own memory.

Old woman, the children say, what matters but the story? Put aside your whining and tell us the story.

I will tell you another story for a moment to relieve the pain of this one.

Aula Leeside, you remember, was famous for her stew. It had a fragrant flavor that no one else could duplicate. One day her neighbor, Etta Peekhole, spied on her stew making. She watched as Aula gathered the little mushrooms that grew in the clover, plucking their little white caps. She watched as she placed them in her stew, and when it had cooked for a long time, Aula plucked the little boiled bodies out. Their flavor had been left in the juices. So that was her secret! Etta Peekhole plucked a few mushrooms of her own, polka-dotted ones, and put them in her stew. She died screaming. The end.

There.

That is better.

You all remember that night, the night that Etra screamed and screamed, how in your fear you sucked the shadows into your mouths. That night, all the little children stopped being children.

In the same way, that day Annakey stopped being a child. It was her soul that screamed. There were no forest shadows anymore, because all the shadows were in her soul. The wild animals that snuffled near the path were stuffed dolls to the wild things that bit away at her heart. She climbed the mountain almost at a run, until she moaned from the pain in her side. She did not stop until she reached the summer meadow. When Annakey reached the outskirts of the summer meadow, she found she could not go in. She could not go to the ones who were keeping the sheep there. She felt that they would be able to smell her shame on her. In the woods outside the summer meadow, she found a fallen tree upon which to sit, and she watched the shepherds through the veil of the forest's edge.

For two days, she sat watching the shepherds at their work, smelling the smoke of their breakfast fires. At night when they were asleep in the sheep shelter, she buried herself beneath the dry leaves of last year's fall. In the day, she watched as an outsider, as one who no longer belonged. On the first day, her food ran out and she did not care. On the second day, she fasted. There was no smile on her face. She made a meadow, and out of twigs and twine she built a sheepcote, not knowing if her heart would let her live to bring it to me. With bits of wool she found caught on thorn bushes around the edges of the meadow, she made each sheep in the meadow. It did not ease her frown.

ON THE THIRD MORNING, Annakey's rage came with her hunger.

She laid aside the sheepcote and began to make a doll, chanting Areth's name as she made it.

The body she made of the black clay mud of the forest

floor. It was a bloated, distorted body, hardly recognizable as human. She wove clothing and hair of twigs and stems. She put a real spider in the doll's head for bad dreams and wicked imaginings, and closed the spider in, alive, with a lump of clay. She pierced her finger with a thorn, and in the chest of the doll she dripped real blood for a wounded heart. In the doll's stomach she placed a worm, and that too she closed in alive. She made arms and legs of sticks, as one who is unable to help himself. She gave the doll no eyes, and especially no mouth.

Annakey was untucking. She was untucking all that she had suffered in her young life, drawing it out of her heart like long slivers. Into the doll she poked small slivers of dried pine needles. Into the doll went all the sadness and hurts, all her hungry nights and her cold days, her lost father and her dead mother and her rage against Areth. The last was so glaring she could see nothing else. She did not know that she had poured all the bitter bits behind her heart into the doll. She called the doll, "Areth."

Annakey set the doll in the crook of a tree and looked at it for a long time.

This was a doll of power.

She looked at her hands in wonder, but the knowledge of her gift was not equal to her sorrow. If she should show this to Dollmage . . . But she would never show this to Dollmage. In its blank face she saw, mute and burning, the wish to return evil for evil. She could not show the doll, but she could put her anger in it.

Just then, she heard a rustling in the bushes. She buried herself in her bed of last year's leaves, thinking to hide herself from a shepherd.

It was two men of the robber people. They came on silent feet and spoke their rough language within her hearing.

Annakey knew her evil doll had drawn them.

Annakey knew also that if they saw the summer meadow, by morning many of the sheep would be gone. The robber people would not care for the sheep. They were hunters only, and excellent thieves. They would steal the sheep, and Annakey's people would be forced to leave their beautiful valley in the spring.

As quietly as she could, Annakey pushed a few leaves onto the doll of the sheepcote she had made. The robber men came closer. She could not yet see them from her lair, but she could hear them laughing low, talking to each other in their strange tongue. She pushed a few more leaves onto the sheepcote, and then a few more. She could see the robber men now, naked but for animal skins, their skin leathered from the sun, for they did not build houses. They lived in caves in the winter and wandered in the summer. Annakey pushed enough leaves onto the sheepcote doll to hide it completely.

The robber men stopped short. They seemed to be lost.

They sat down near enough to Annakey that she could hear their talk. The robber people have a different language than the valley people, of course, but since the coming of our people we have learned some few words of their language. From her hiding place Annakey could see the robber men gesturing down toward her village and using the word "beautiful" and laughing. She knew that the robber people had a plan to steal women from the village.

A beetle crawled on Annakey's arm, but she did not care, for a spider crawled in her heart. Around her neck hung her promise doll, and it was speaking to her. "Did you not promise to save your people? You must not die."

After a little time the robber men stood and continued on

their way, in the opposite direction from which they had
come. The summer meadow with its sheep was safe for now.
The robber men would return to their people and tell them
they had scouted this part of the forest and had found nothing. They would not come this way again for a long time.

Annakey emerged from her bed of leaves. She looked up
at the evil doll she had made, still hanging in the tree. She
could either live or hate, not both. There was no time for hating right now. She knocked it out of the tree and kicked
some dirt and leaves over it.

Annakey said aloud. "You are the Evil doll. Stay here,
buried on the mountain, for I will not have evil follow me."

Annakey began her trek back to the village.

EVEN IN MY ELOQUENCE I am unable to tell you how
Annakey felt at that time. I can tell you, however, that as
Annakey began her walk back down to the village, carrying
the sheepcote doll, she saw the mayster robins red among the
green leaves, and the fulsome bluejays. She saw the fine, manly
forest and the lady sky, she smelled the peppernut smell of
leaves turning to dust, she heard the chatter of birds and the fall
of water on rocks. I can tell you that Annakey's heart decided
to live. I can tell you that Annakey was no longer afraid.

I SAW ANNAKEY NEXT standing in my doorway, leaves in her
wild hair, and thin and pale as a wood nymph. I had not made
her comfortable enough in my house for her to come in
without invitation as Renoa did, and so she stood there.

"Manal was ready to go look for you, but Areth came down
from the mountain saying that you had promised to marry
him. He forbade Manal to look for you. Is it true, Annakey?"

Her chest rose as if she would speak, but no word came

out. When she did not answer, I said, "When you did not come, Areth told Manal that it was taking you longer to make the sheepcote doll than you had anticipated. Manal insisted upon looking for you, but Areth told him it would be unseemly to go looking for a girl who belonged to someone else. The village elders agreed."

In Annakey's arms was the doll of the summer meadow and the sheepcote. She looked at me silently, begging me to see what I would not see.

"Greppa Lowmeadow has announced that your wedding day will take place on the same day that Renoa is named Dollmage. It is strange. I thought you loved Manal. . . . Ah. This is why you took so long. It is good," I said, and took the sheepcote greedily from her arms. It pleasured me to look at her work. Somehow it was sweeter, the way a meal is sweeter when prepared by hands other than your own.

"I will add my power to it," I said.

"There is no need, Dollmage. Can you not see?" She reminded me so much of Vilsa at that moment. Her presumption took all the joy out of my seeing. She had lost her fear of me. Then she said, "Manal believed that I agreed to marry Areth?"

"He did not believe him, until Areth described your breasts to him."

Annakey clutched at her promise doll. Her head hung, and I could not see her face for her wild hair. "What did Manal do?"

"A strange thing," I said, looking closely at the sheepcote. I could find no imperfections. "He began to build a house. He is not supposed to build a house until I have built it for the village doll. I will not punish him under the law. I see that his madness is a result of his suffering."

Finally, she raised her head. Her mouth was not smiling. It was clamped shut, as if she were carrying a great burden. I looked into her eyes. What was it about her eyes? I wanted to be pleased that finally her frowning doll had won and vindicated my powers, but what was it about her eyes?

"You say he is building?" she asked.

"Yes."

"A house?"

"Yes," I answered irritably, adding, "I have warned him it will fall unless I have made the doll of it first, but he builds tirelessly."

What was it in her eyes?

"Dollmage," she said, "Areth came upon me in the mountains and . . . and violated me."

So. So. That was what was in her eyes: a sadness too deep. You must believe me, I had not wanted her to frown at such a price.

"You must go to the House of Women and ask for justice," I said at last, and quietly.

She nodded and closed her eyes and I saw her eyelids tremble. "My second promise, Dollmage, was to save my people. The robber people—I know they plan next to steal a woman. Let me help you make a plan to save our people."

"Make your contest doll," I said.

"The villagers must be warned," she said. "None of the women or children should go out alone. . . . Tell them."

"Common sense tells them that."

"Please," Annakey said.

"Very well. I will go to Weeper's Stump today." Then my heart reached out to her and I said, "Before you begin your doll for the contest, I have another thing for you to do."

She had turned away. Now she turned back again.

"Would you leave Manal vulnerable? I want you to make a doll of his house and bring it to me. Who knows what will happen if he continues?"

I could scarcely see her face in the twilight. She knew I had asked her to do this out of compassion for her. "I will do it," she said, "but you must know, I will not keep my promise to Areth."

"A promise breaker can never be Dollmage," I said.

"Why do you say that, if there is no danger that I will be Dollmage?" she asked.

I stammered a moment, and then said, "A promise breaker is in danger of her life."

"There are worse things than dying," she said.

"That is why your promise doll frowns," I called after her, for she was walking away from me. "It frowns in disapproval over a broken promise."

Annakey disappeared into the twilight. I heard Manal's saw make a long, hard song until past dark.

THAT NIGHT ANNAKEY went to the House of Women. The men endured the House of Women out of long tradition and feared it a little. Men are the bosses. Even I, as Dollmage, have no say as to what crop will go where, or when to build a new plough or who will attend to the hunt and who to the fences. They do not ask me. But we have, in the House of Women, done a thing or two. Once, it came out in the House that Dug Shallowslough was hitting his wife. Each woman went home and did not please her man until he told Dug to hit no one less hairy than himself. Dug was the hairiest man in the village. He became a very peaceful man.

As I said, that night Annakey went to the House of Women. Grandmother Keepmoney sat at the door, stick in hand. She stood up and held the stick out to prevent Annakey from entering.

"You may not enter," Grandmother Keepmoney said.

Annakey stood still, unbelieving. "Why?"

"It is my duty to prevent the unworthy."

"You never prevent anyone."

"Tonight I do."

Annakey swallowed. "How am I unworthy?"

Grandmother Keepmoney put her stick down and leaned on it. "Greppa Lowmeadow says that you came to her and said you would not keep your promise to marry her son Areth with whom you have shared your body."

Annakey's head bent as if her promise doll were dragging it down. "No. That is why I have come, to ask for justice. I did not share. I was forced."

Grandmother Keepmoney put up her stick again wearily. "So you say. I hear otherwise."

"From who?"

"Areth Lowmeadow himself."

"Have you ever known me to lie, Grandmother Keepmoney?"

"Perhaps you do not know what is real, child."

Annakey stared. The old woman looked at her and her face drew down and her shoulders sagged.

"I believe you, child. Some will not. It does not matter. I cannot let you in, a promise breaker. Only deny that you have broken your promise, and I will let you in."

Annakey said nothing.

Grandmother Keepmoney said, "Grave consequences will come of this, Annakey. The people are afraid, and they speak as if they want to take their fear out on you."

"I will ask Areth to release me from my promise," Annakey

said. Then, because Grandmother Keepmoney still guarded the door, she walked away.

MY PEOPLE.

Now you understand much.

Will you forgive Annakey, free her, ask for her forgiveness?

No, perhaps not, but I see you do not touch your stones so lovingly. No matter. Even if you are persuaded, Areth will let fly his stone, and that is enough to kill her. Now that the truth is out and he has lost the respect of his people, he has nothing to lose. You see as I do that he will kill Annakey, and anyone in the way of that rock. You forget, though, that I have a secret still.

Yes, Manal, rub her wrists, and give her bread to eat.

Why, you ask, for she has broken a promise and brought this fate upon our village. What good is bread to a dead girl?

That is true.

That I cannot deny.

Nevertheless, listen on.

THAT NIGHT I STARED at the sheepcote a long time. How old I felt, how pressed down and part of the earth I felt. Then I saw, in one of the trees of the sheepcote doll, a tiny nest, and in it, three almost invisible eggs. I could not stop the welling tears.

I went to Areth Lowmeadow.

"Will you release her?" I asked, low and in the dark.

"No," he said.

"If you do not, she may die."

"Let her die," he said.

"Is this your love?" I asked, and then I grasped his promise doll in my hand. I took my carving knife and slashed it across his doll, once, between the head and the body.

"What have you done?" he whined pitifully.

"Only what you have done to another's heart," I said.

"But I am within the law."

"That is not what I hear."

"She is a liar."

"Then you need not fear," I said.

When I arrived home I took my husband's ghost doll and put it near my house in the village model. Now, now I was ready to die.

[Chapter 10]

INSCRIPTION ON THE LOVE DOLL:
*It is God's plan that love so meant can be
eternal covenant.*

THE NEXT DAY Manal was early at his house. For days he had
hauled logs. He had paced off the size of the house on the
ground, and with his spade he dug a shallow hollow along
two sides of that space. Into each of the hollows he rolled his
biggest logs, the sills. That was when I stopped him, forbade
him to do any more until a doll was made of his house. He
contented himself with making notches at the ends of the
logs with his ax. The villagers plied him with questions. Why
would an unmarried man build a house? Which of the
rumors were true about Annakey? He ignored everyone, and
so they began to question his mother, Norda Bantercross.
Norda also ignored them and made a great business about
sewing curtains and quilts and cushions for her son's new
house.

That morning, Manal stopped sawing when Annakey
came and sat down beside his house with her materials.

"Annakey." His voice was gentle. Manal, too, was grown
wise.

"Dollmage has asked me to build the doll of your house,"
Annakey said. These were the first words she had spoken to
him since she had discovered the Evil doll with her own

hands. How strange words sounded to her, now that she no longer had the same mouth. With new eyes, the sun seemed too bright and all the birds sounded tinny and shrill. There was nothing to protect her if he said the wrong thing.

"You have already built me a house in your own valley doll," he said. "That is the house I want."

"Dollmage does not know. I will pretend to build a house, and then I will go fetch the other."

"This keeps you from making your contest doll," Manal said.

"Manal, why did you not come to the summer meadow with me?" she asked.

"I was not told you were going," he said.

Annakey looked up. "But Renoa said she would tell you. . . ." Then she lowered her voice. "You must not believe all the stories Areth will tell you, that others will tell you. . . ."

"I know you."

Annakey closed her eyes and nodded. Then she knelt and began to work with the materials she had brought. "Manal, one thing is true. It is true that I promised myself to Areth, but—"

"You love me."

"I do." Annakey shook her head. "He was going to . . . to hurt me, and so . . . I promised to . . . marry him."

"Then some of the stories are true. Now I will hurt him." Manal leapt to his feet.

Annakey put her hand on his. "If you do so, it will not help me, and it will divide and destroy our village. I will not marry Areth. I have already broken the promise in my heart. But what will I do? If I break a promise, I cannot be Dollmage. If I am not Dollmage—Manal, listen—I cannot keep my first promise to be happy. Manal, what have I done?"

Manal was silent for a time, gathering himself.

"We will run away," he said. "You will be my Dollmage."

Annakey shook her head. "What of my promise to save the village from the robber people?"

Manal thought for a moment, and then said, "I, too, am a man of his promise, and I have promised myself to you, Annakey. That is all that is clear to me now. It is you I will love, whether you are married to me or not, and it is for you I build this house, whether you live in it or not."

"I will make it right, Manal. I will make your house and a story for it."

The two began to work in silence then. It was enough to know that the other was near. When it was time to eat, Manal brought her food. They were eating when Areth came by.

"What is this?" he asked.

Annakey felt a worm in her stomach, seeing Areth again. "Dollmage set me to make a doll of Manal's new house," she said.

"You will not eat with another man when you are prom- ised to me," Areth said.

Annakey stood. I will not tell you what Manal's expression was at that moment. I will tell you that Areth wanted to walk away from it, and he did. Annakey gestured to Manal to stay behind, then caught up with Areth, the bread still in her hand.

"I do not want you to eat his food," Areth said.

She took a bite and chewed and swallowed. "Areth, I have something to say to you."

"You told Dollmage," he said. He held up his slashed promise doll. "This is what she did to me." He turned and walked away, and Annakey followed. He turned to her and said, "Why do you follow me?"

"I must speak to you."

"Go away. I cannot bear the sight of you."

"Areth," she said, "does that mean you release me from my promise?"

He laughed, his eyes as hard as those of the War doll. "I do not release you."

"But you do not love me."

"No. I hate you. The sight of you makes me sick."

"Once, we were friends," she said.

"Do not use your gentle ways with me," he said, and his hand fisted. "You have hurt me. I know you now to be evil. If I find you again with Manal, I will kill you."

Annakey stood shaking, her lips gray. "I will tell Dollmage you threatened to kill me. She will find a way to release me from my promise."

"I will deny what I have said."

"You would lie?"

"You would break your promise to me? Who possesses the greater evil, Annakey? I have known, perhaps since we were children together, that you were a promise breaker." His voice was rising, and the muscles in his neck protruded.

"Then you do not know me."

"I know you. I know you better than Manal knows you. I know your heart to be evil."

"Let me go then, Areth."

He slapped her face. "You have promised yourself to me, and you belong to me. I have told the whole village. Now, go away from me."

Annakey stepped back. The blood in her heart was black. "I followed you to tell you I will not marry you," she said, her voice shaking.

Areth's lips were gray. "Then my mother spoke true when she said you would break your promise?"

"I have already," Annakey said, gasping. "I will never marry you. Tell whom you will. I would rather die."

ANNAKEY RAN HARD to her secret place beside the rushy river, to fetch the true doll of Manal's house. First, she listened to the river shushing her heart. She began to touch the pale green clay in the river shallows.

On the great, flat rock was her valley doll, and in it, her village doll. She had made the valley over and over, striving to get it right. She had made it in fall, the fog knee-deep in the golden wood, the berries glossy on the bush. She had made the valley in winter, the snows deep to the tree trunks, the green mosses turned to gray. Now, however, as she looked at it in its spring, she saw that it was still not quite Seekvalley. It was different—a distortion. She could gather no happiness from it, seeing that it was wrong. What could she have been thinking? Had she no eye to see? It did not occur to Annakey that she was taking the story of the village entirely from me. She did not think it was good enough.

She could not work on it today. She leaned over the river and took from its bottom more of the smooth, green clay. She began to fashion the doll of a bear. When Annakey finished the doll of the bear, she made a wildcat. After a time she breathed deeply, and smiled just a little. Enough to keep her first promise. She knew what she would do to save her people.

There was no time now. She had to return with the doll of Manal's house and report to me. Just before she left, she saw something floating in the river. It floated into the quiet little bay at her feet.

It was the Evil doll she had made and left buried in leaves at the summer meadow.

The worm in her stomach twisted again. A spider in her head tickled her brain. How did the Evil doll come here? Did one of the sheepdogs pick it up and drop it into the river? Her arms were stiff as sticks as she watched it bobbing in the water. Finally, she reached down and picked it up.

She carried the doll of Manal's house and the Evil doll into the tame parts of the valley.

She buried the Evil doll in Fatbarley's field.

Then she went to Manal's house and set about improving upon the doll of it. She did not see Manal watching her, stopping his work to look at her. She was trying to forget the drowned face of the Evil doll by working hard. She built the chimney strong and safe, and the floors without creaks. She made the doors solid against the winter winds, and stone walls cool against the summer heat. I tell you that she tried to build a place for her soul to hide.

It did not work.

Renoa came to her as twilight was coming on.

"I have almost finished my contest doll," she said. "And you?"

"I have not begun yet," Annakey said. "First light, I will begin."

"Are you sure this is not your attempt?" Renoa asked.

In her hands was the Evil doll.

"How did you—?"

"A pig dug it up in Fatbarley's field and deposited at the door of his house. He took it as an omen. I know you made it. Who else could make such a monstrosity? I am going to show Dollmage."

"No, Renoa, please."

"When Dollmage and the villagers see this, there will no longer be any need for a contest."

Annakey put her hands on either side of her head. The spider in her head was making her imagine pushing Renoa.

Manal approached the girls, sweating from his work.

"Look what Annakey has done," Renoa said to him. "Are you sure you want her making your house?"

Annakey stood. She could not look at Manal for fear that there would be disappointment in his eyes.

"The doll is you, Renoa," Manal said. "I see a resemblance."

Renoa glared and grabbed Annakey's arm. "We are going to see Dollmage."

"I can explain," Annakey said, pulling back.

"Explain to Dollmage," she said.

They both came to my house, but I was asleep.

"Stay here the night," Renoa said to Annakey. "At first light we must show Dollmage what you have done."

WHEN RENOA WAS ASLEEP, Annakey took the doll to the village bakery oven. She threw the doll into the bottom of the oven below the grills, and closed the door.

IN THE MORNING there came a desperate knocking at my door, waking me. It was Deen Highchimney.

"Come to my house, Dollmage. My wife is hysterical."

Prim Highchimney had been on the verge of hysteria ever since she had finally become pregnant after five years of marriage. Every tiny thing made her weep. I was still too sleepy to wonder why Annakey was in my kitchen peeling rutabagas. Renoa was still asleep. I nodded to Annakey. "Go. See what Prim weeps over this time. If it is a great thing, come for me and I will deal with it. I suspect she needs comforting only."

Annakey went.

At the Highchimneys' door, Prim stood trembling. In her hands was a large loaf of bread, broken open. In the bread was the Evil doll.

"I was going into the mountain today to pray for my child that has not been born," she said. "As I prepared a meal to bring, I found this. God is telling me I am going to have an ugly baby, a monster child."

Annakey snatched up the Evil doll. The Evil doll was more hideous even than before. The fire had burned into the face what could be taken as eyes and a mouth.

"No, Prim, do not be sad. This has nothing to do with you." She lowered her voice. "Would you like me to make a pregnancy doll for you, Prim? I will make it the most beautiful baby. Only you must say nothing of this thing you found in your bread."

Prim smiled wanly. "I asked Dollmage to make a pregnancy doll for me, but she said she was too old and her powers too weak. She said to wait until the contest decided things and then Renoa would make one for me. Will you make it today?"

Annakey swallowed. If she made it today, when would she make her contest doll?

"I will make it today," she said.

She looked at the Evil doll as she walked away, and almost called it "Renoa." Renoa was the source of all her trouble and her unhappiness. She threw the doll into the river, watched it float downstream, and returned to my house.

Renoa was still sleeping when Annakey returned to the house. When she awoke she looked for the Evil doll, but it was gone. She tried to explain to me that Annakey had made a monster doll, but when I asked Annakey about it, she told me she had thrown it in the river. "It was a mistake," she said. I was too busy to press her further and so I dropped it, but I could see Renoa haunting her all day about it.

All morning, Annakey worked on a doll. She was secretive. She would not let me see it. Toward noon, she disappeared with it.

"In the morning," I called after her. "In the morning, I will see your contest doll anyway."

At the Highchimneys' house, only Deen was there.

"I have the pregnancy doll finished," Annakey said.

Deen looked at it and smiled and nodded. "It is just like her," he said.

"Where is she?"

"She has gone to the mountain to pray that her child will not be ugly."

"Deen! Alone?"

"Alone."

"But the robber people . . . Did not Dollmage go to Weeper's Stump to tell the people not to go out of the village alone?"

Deen frowned. "Dollmage has not stood on Weeper's Stump since last spring."

"But the robber people . . . Could you not realize of yourself how dangerous it would be to let her go alone?"

Deen's frown turned to fear. "I told her not to go, but she would not listen to me. I wanted to go with her, but she refused, said it was women's worship."

Annakey ran outside and stood looking into the near mountain, the pregnancy doll hanging from her hand.

"When did she say she would return?" Annakey demanded.

Deen shook his head. He was almost crying now. "She said she would be back in time to make my dinner, and now it is almost suppertime."

Annakey dropped the pregnancy doll and ran to my house.

Of course I called together all the men of the village and we began to search for her. I saw the accusation in Annakey's eyes when she told me that Prim was late coming home from her pilgrimage. She had told me to warn the villagers at Weeper's Stump and I had not. Was it my fault that a villager could be so stupid? No, it was God's Fault, capital *F*.

We searched until the sunlight failed and then we searched in the twilight. It was Annakey that saw Prim running along a narrow path cut into the cliffside of the mountain face opposite us. She called out. Prim saw us, stopped, and then, with a glance behind her, continued running as fast as her pregnant body would let her. Only then did we see two robber men pursuing her.

The men of the search party screamed threats at the robber men. When they were almost upon her, Prim lost her footing and fell.

She did not die. Some feet below her was a gravel shelf, and there she lay, out of reach of the robber men. They turned back, and were gone by the time we came to her.

Prim was bruised about her bottom, and for that reason I did not bruise her bottom myself. That night she was delivered of twins, a boy and a girl. At dawn, half of you were outside her door waiting to see the babies.

"There. You see there was nothing to worry about," I said to Prim.

"It is because of the pregnancy doll Annakey made for us," Deen said in his joy. He held it up for me to see. Some of you villagers were peering in the door.

"This is your contest doll?" I asked.

"No," Annakey said, "I have not had time yet to make my contest doll."

"Dollmage, Annakey made us a doll and now all is well. Is she not your successor then?" Prim asked weakly.

"It was not her pregnancy doll but mine that made everything well," Renoa said.

She stood in the doorway, having elbowed her way through to the front. The new day's light was behind her so that her face was in shadow. "You said the contest would be over in the morning, Dollmage. It is morning. This is the contest doll I made. It is a pregnancy doll for Prim."

I looked at the doll. It, too, was good.

I looked at the curious faces of the villagers in the door and windows, and those behind craning their necks to see. "How can I tell whose doll is responsible for delivering Prim safely?" I said aloud.

"Judge you, Dollmage," Renoa said. "Look inside my pregnancy doll."

I took the baby out of her pregnancy doll, and then in delight saw that there was another baby inside. "Twins, Renoa. You promised her twins!"

The whispers of the crowd grew to murmurs.

Renoa smiled in triumph at Annakey. "How many babies are there in Annakey's doll?"

I looked. "Only one," I said. "A boy. There is the contest. Renoa, you are my successor."

"But . . . but that was not meant to be my contest doll," Annakey stammered. "I only made it to help Prim—"

"What does it matter?" Renoa said. "Finally we have seen that I am the true Dollmage."

I faced the crowd.

"There will be a feast. Annakey, at the feast you must promise that from now on you will not make any dolls."

Annakey glanced up at the mountains.

"What about the robber people?" she asked. "I have a plan. If you will only let me do one more thing."

"I have proof enough, now, Annakey," I said gently. "Be humbled. Come, and serve your new Dollmage."

What was in Annakey's eyes at that moment? I told myself she was merely sad to lose.

"I see now that this is why God gave you a frowning promise doll—because you were going to be sad to lose."

"Dollmage," she said, "if only you will let me make the dolls necessary to chase the robber people away."

"Come, Renoa," I said, going out the door.

Renoa followed, and so also did Annakey. I did not stop to hear her, but she followed me, protesting all the time. It was shameful that she would degrade herself so, and I said as much. "Remember your promise to be happy—"

I stopped short. A wail was coming from the house of Deen and Prim Highchimney. A wail, oh, the wail of unspeakable pain, and it did not stop, no, it did not stop, not even when I rushed back into the house to see what was the trouble.

This was the trouble: Prim's baby girl had died.

[Chapter 11]

INSCRIPTION ON THE MERCY DOLL:
*Wherever possible, the people will try to
extend mercy to the wrongdoer.*

NOW WHO WAS THE DOLLMAGE? I ask you. Was it the one who made twin babies in the pregnancy doll? Twins were born. Or was it the one who made a baby boy? The boy lived. Now, some of you already feared Annakey. Had she, in her carelessness, caused the baby girl to die? Had she drowned Rolly the cow and burned Follownot the sheep? Why was it something bad happened every time Annakey made a doll? And were the rumors true that she was a promise breaker? While Prim wailed her voice into a whimper and a whisper, the villagers conferred with me. They wanted me to name Renoa as Dollmage.

"Have I not been telling you all along?" I asked, but I said it without conviction. I said it, remembering the rubber boots and the bees in Wifebury's potting shed. I said it, remembering the sheepcote. I said it, remembering that I had created your fear of Annakey.

"Dollmage," said Annakey, "please. I have a plan. Only give me a little longer and I will chase away the robber people." Her face was pale. She swallowed over and over.

"Hush," I said. She thought I meant her, but I meant everyone. "Hush. The full moon is not until tonight. Annakey will have until moonrise to make her contest doll."

There was a silence and then an outcry. I held up a hand and pointed to a high, treeless ridge. There stood a party of robber people, at least fifty strong. When the robber people organize enough to gather themselves, it is grave danger. The outcry ceased. A few women ran for their children. Wifebury put his finger and thumb into the sockets of his eyes, then looked again, blinking.

I spoke urgently to Annakey, in the hearing of all of you. "Until dusk I give you to make your contest doll." I could hear muffled weeping somewhere in the village, and then more. It grew until it was a chorus of weeping.

"Tell them to be silent and brave, or they shall have my wrath," I hissed to the men.

The crowd dispersed. Annakey ran away on silent feet.

"Stupid woman," Renoa said to me. "Why cannot you make up your mind?"

It broke my heart to have her say so. I had let her be proud and venomous to others, and now she was spending her venom on me. "You speak to me so, Renoa?" I said haughtily.

"You know I am your successor," she said.

"You are. So, do you have a plan, as Annakey does, to save the village from the robber people?"

"I have a plan. It is for you to give me all the relics of your power. I will move into your house, and it will be my house, and the dolls will be mine, and you will go away from me, where you cannot suck the magic out of me like an old leech. You are old, Dollmage. That is why the village is not safe. It is because you are old, and your powers are gone."

Then I knew. It was as she was speaking to me that I knew how it was the robber people could find us, even when the village doll was hidden from them.

"The village doll is no longer making the story," I said, more to myself than to Renoa. "I see it now. Annakey must have her own village doll somewhere. That is where she is going, even now."

"She could not do it. She is not the Dollmage. I am."

Annakey was indeed running to her secret place. If she made her contest doll and it did not win, she knew that she would be made to promise not to fashion any doll ever again. She touched the clay bear and the clay wildcat she had made. Perhaps an apronful of wild animal dolls could not win the contest. She decided then that if only she had time to do one thing, she would keep her second promise to save her people. As soon as she decided that, she found she had kept her first promise to her mother: that she would be happy.

Why did she desire above all to save you? I told you once it was because she loved you as a people for keeping your promises. That is only part of it. It was also because she saw that she must—that no one else could do it for you, that I was old and Renoa was careless, and all of you depended upon her ability to devise a plan. She wanted to save you because she could, and because her own life depended upon it.

All afternoon Annakey worked with clay and other things that her secret bower provided. This was her plan: Around her village doll on the large, flat rock, she would place dolls of the robber people. Then, around each of the dolls of the robber people, she would place clay bears and wildcats and wolves also. She would summon the wild animals with her dolls to chase away the robber people from our village. She would warn the villagers to stay in their houses for a few days, and when she was sure the robber people were all gone, she would remove the wild animals from around the village model.

She had worked a long time when she heard someone running through the forest. Manal burst upon her secret bower.

"Come," he said. "Dollmage said I must fetch you."

"Manal, I am not yet finished."

"It is dusk, Annakey, the whole village is looking for you. The robber people have taken Oda Weedbridge. Even Dollmage is frightened. The wolves are baying, and cats are screaming from every mountain. Dollmage is standing on Weeper's Stump, sending people farther and farther afield until you come. I am worried that someone will stray too close to the robber people looking for you, or be eaten by wild animals."

Annakey shook. She glanced up at the sky. Had so much time passed? She had no contest doll, and she had not yet saved her people. Her only hope was to go to Dollmage, instruct the people to hide in their homes, and ask for a little more time. Manal and Annakey held hands as they rushed back to the village. The wolves were howling.

As she walked into the village, you who had been looking for her stopped your search and followed her. Almost the entire village was at Weeper's Stump when Annakey arrived.

As soon as I saw Annakey, I raised my hand and the villagers fell silent. "The robber people have taken an old woman. Next time it will be a young woman, and then children. The people demand that I name my successor. We can wait no longer, Annakey. Where is your contest doll?"

Annakey held out her hands to me as if she were hoping a doll would appear there by magic. "Give me more time. Please."

"No more time," I said. "What have you been doing?"

Annakey looked up. "Dollmage, come and see. I have no

contest doll, but if you see the work of my hands at a secret place of mine where I have devised a plan to repel the robber people—"

"No," said Renoa. "The time is up. By her own admission, she has no contest doll."

All of you murmured, as you remember well, and I held up my hand for silence.

"What secret place?" I asked.

"In the forest, where the river comes out of the mountain. I have made my own valley doll there, and a village doll in it. If only you will give me a little more time, I can rid us of the robber people."

Again you murmured. Again I silenced you. It was as I suspected. "It is a long way for me to walk, but I must." It was Annakey's story, now. I was resigned.

Renoa strode forward. "No."

"Out of envy you say so," Manal said to Renoa.

"You think Annakey is good," Renoa cried. "I will prove to you that she is evil. She made this!"

Then Renoa held up the Evil doll that Annakey had made.

It was hideous now, having been twice drowned and bitten by animals and burned and buried.

"I found it by the riverbank," Renoa said. "Prim will witness that Annakey herself made this monstrosity."

I stared at the doll, and all the village stared at the doll, and Annakey stared at the doll. For a long time, the only sound was that of the swans trumpeting on the river.

"Did you make this?" I asked at last.

Annakey looked at Renoa. She wanted to lie, but to lie is to break the promise of words, and Annakey would not do that. In that moment, her heart bled, wounded, and in her stomach the worm made her stomach sick. Her arms and legs were as heavy as deadwood, and a spider in her brain bit at the backs of her eyes so they ached and watered.

Greppa Lowmeadow stepped forward then. "It is the doll of Annakey's heart, for she has broken her promise to marry my son, Areth. Deny it, if you can."

She did not deny.

There was a general moaning and protestation from the crowd. Those of you who had refused to believe the gossip spoke out in disbelief. In all your lives you had never seen a promise broken. In the stories, those who did so ran away into the mountains and joined the robber people rather than be stoned.

I held up my hand.

Not taking my eyes from the doll, I asked, "Did you make this, Annakey?"

She did not hesitate. "Yes," she said.

"What is this doll, Annakey? What does it mean?"

Annakey opened her mouth to speak, and closed it. She looked around at her people. For the first time, Annakey knew what the doll meant, who the doll was.

She had made it a vessel for the injustice done her, the hurts and the bad things that had happened to her. Now Annakey knew that the doll kept coming back to her because she was still holding all the anger and hurts inside her. Deep down, she knew now, was anger that her father, and then her mother, had left her. Deep down, in places behind her heart, were hates for Renoa and for Areth, and for me. Powerful hates. And Annakey knew now that they would eat at her brain like a spider and at her stomach like a worm until she rid herself of them. She knew her anger and hate would eat at her heart, bleeding it to death. She knew that she would be powerless and blind and voiceless unless she could rid herself of her hate.

"I call it 'Evil doll'," Annakey said, so quietly I could scarcely hear her.

"Evil doll," I said, echoing her words in barely a whisper. I knew it was true. As I looked at it, I saw it was me, me, me, and then, looking ashamed into the eyes of all of you, I saw that each one of you saw it as yourself.

Then Annakey spoke into the silence. "Look carefully, Dollmage. Look. The doll is . . . me."

All of you murmured in agreement. "Yes," you said, "yes." You wanted it to be Annakey and not yourselves.

"Annakey," she said. "The doll's name is 'Annakey.' "

"So I must be Dollmage," Renoa said. "Declare it now, before all."

Annakey looked at Manal, and he looked back and smiled comfortingly. The crowd began to jabber again as Manal began to lead Annakey away.

"Wait, Annakey!" I called.

Annakey waited.

I took the Evil doll from her and held it up to all of you. "There is evil in all of us," I said. "The way to overcoming the evil in us is to recognize it, to draw it out before our eyes and examine it in the light of day. With this doll, Annakey has done just that. This doll has power. This doll shows more power than any doll I have made in my lifetime. It . . . it will be a Sacred doll."

As soon as I said this, as soon as I let go of my pride, God spoke to me and opened my eyes and let me see my art.

I looked slowly around at you villagers. You need not use your memory dolls to remember what was said so shortly ago. "Annakey's mother, Vilsa, was my cousin. Likely there was magic in her blood." I said it to myself, but all of you heard. Your every eye was upon me, waiting. "If I had been better, I should have named her my successor years before my husband died. Now, I will tell you about Annakey's promise doll. For the first time I understand, and I am not afraid of it. The hole in her promise doll signifies the hole the world makes in her heart, through which she feels the weight of the world every day. She must bear the weight of it, as a Doll-mage does. If her heart had not been strong, the world would have pulled through, ripping the flesh like an earring torn from the ear. She would have died from a broken heart. Just as her doll hangs crookedly, so will the world be bent slant-a-ways just a little, because of her heart. It will not allow the world to hang like a heavy stone. Her heart will rock it side to side, tip it up on its end.

"Furthermore, the reason her promise doll frowns is not because she is destined to be unhappy, and not because she is not the Dollmage. It is because her promise doll does not always get its way. She will have power over her own destiny, and her destiny is that she will be happy. She will be Doll-mage.

"Annakey, in the eyes of all these witnesses, you I name my successor. Annakey, you are Dollmage."

[Chapter 12]

RENOA PULLED HER PROMISE DOLL from around her neck and made a loud hissing sound. She held it high for all to see, she shoved it in my face. Her teeth were clamped, her lips pulled back. We all fell silent as she shook her promise doll in all our faces. Then she put it back on, slowly, ceremoniously, defying every glance with a glare. Finally, she said to me, "Vile old woman. All my life you have the robbed the power out of me. Only when I was away from you could I feel my strength as a Dollmage. Now I will be Dollmage. I will, for I will no longer let you feed on my power, not even long enough to name another Dollmage."

She stood looking at me, hating me as much as she had loved me. I turned away from her and said, "Be Dollmage, Annakey. Love and lead your people, and make their stories with all the art of your hands, and make them true totems of promise."

Annakey nodded.

Cries came, "But what of the broken promise?"

"Yes, Dollmage," Greppa Lowmeadow said, "if Annakey is to be Dollmage, she must keep all her promises." She put her arm around Renoa, who said nothing. She was clutching her promise doll so tightly that the thong dug into the flesh at her neck.

"That is so," I said.

"Before you declare her Dollmage, you should see that she keep her promise to marry me," Areth said.

"Dollmage," Annakey said, "has God provided no way?"

I touched her shoulder. "God always provides a way. It is one of the things that makes me his friend," I said.

Renoa's face became gray. She released her grip on her promise doll.

"You, Hobblefoot. I know your secret," she shrieked. "You yourself are a promise breaker, for I have seen your husband's ghost wandering in the forests, and I have spoken to him. Now I will find him and bring him to you so you can die." The crowd, utterly baffled and afraid, said nothing. Their eyes were more upon the ridge than upon me. She slipped away on bare feet. She did not see my husband, already amongst the crowd.

I said nothing to defend myself. The first promise broken leads to the next until there is no end.

"I have searched the Sacred dolls," I said to Annakey. "As a villager, you can be released from your promise to marry Areth. The death of your heart the day that Areth hurt you is a fair enough price. But it is different for a Dollmage. Your promise can be broken only at the price of a death. If you are dead, however, you can keep none of your other promises. Areth must release you from your promise to him. Where is Areth?"

Areth was nowhere to be seen, and so some went to find him.

As I waited, I saw storm clouds on the horizon and hoped for rain, and sun by morning.

NOW, RENOA HAD RUN AWAY to the end of the valley. In the half-light she came to where the great trees hang down their long branches to pinch and scratch, to the place where there are eyes in every hole and under every leaf. She came to the place where the river runs out of the mountain, where the wild things come to wash their bloody whiskers in the water. Renoa came to Annakey's secret place.

On the huge, flat rock she saw Annakey's doll of Seekvalley, and beside it all the wild animals Annakey had formed of clay.

"So!" she said aloud and to no one.

She walked around the large, flat rock slowly, looking and looking but not touching. "So," she said again, "Hobblefoot was right. This is why the village is no longer hidden by the sky blanket."

Then Renoa thought of a way to destroy Annakey.

Why? you ask. Because those who would hurt others do not care for themselves. It is true for myself as well. I was unsure of my powers as a Dollmage. This made me feel less about myself. That made me want to have the powers of a Dollmage even more. Which made me angry when I thought that Annakey's promise doll was not keeping its promise. Only to the extent that I despised myself could I despise Annakey.

Now my confession is almost full. I hope that makes God happy. It is my deep desire that we are friends.

Still smoldering in the secret bower was the little fire that Annakey had built before Manal found her. Renoa took the mosses and twigs and branches and bark that made the village, and dumped them into the fire. Quickly the moss caught fire, and soon the whole doll was in flames.

Then Renoa gathered the little wild animals into her apron and headed back to the village.

We were all still standing together in the village common, watching as more robber men gathered on the mountain ridge. They had begun to stamp their feet rhythmically, when Renoa came running to me.

"Look, Dollmage. Look what I have made," Renoa called as she ran to me. She poured the clay animals, the treecats and the bears, the wolves and the panthers, all onto the ground from her apron. "Are they not wonderful? Can you not sense in them a power also? Name me Dollmage. Name me!"

"Renoa, my wild animals—," Annakey said.

"Not yours," Renoa said. "Mine. I made them. Dollmage, you sense the power in her Evil doll, but do you not remember that she made the doll? She has evil in her enough to lie. I made the animals."

"Take them away from here," Annakey said. She looked around frantically. "Give them to me, Renoa. I will take them to the edge of the wood."

Renoa grasped them to her and backed away. "Leave me alone. You stole my birthright. I was to be the Dollmage. I was due to be born that day. Your mother was early. I have the smiling promise doll."

"Renoa," I said, trying to quiet her, for now I knew what Annakey feared. If the dolls indeed had power, they would draw the wild animals to the village. The snarl of a panther cat rang through the valley. It was close at the forest's edge. "Renoa, it is too late. I have made Annakey the Dollmage. Give her the clay animals," I said.

Renoa sobbed once.

"My Renoa, be comforted. It is possible that she is to die for her broken promise."

You see how well I knew you?

Renoa backed away. "They are mine."

Annakey lunged at her, and Renoa ran. Before anyone could follow her, two men came running, breathless and almost weeping.

"Robber people . . . the crops . . . We cannot stop it. . . ."

"What is it?" I asked, and then I saw what everyone else had already seen by now. What had been storm clouds on the east horizon were now clouds of black smoke.

"The robber people have set fire to the crops," one of the men said. "The forest is afire now too. We cannot stop it. There is a grassfire in the valley. It is coming toward the village. . . ."

"Everyone, go into the river!" I cried. "Bring blankets, anything to wet and cover yourselves. Hurry!"

"You first, Dollmage," Annakey said, grasping my arm.

"No. I will try to find Renoa."

Annakey and Manal ran to help those with many children. I went in the direction I had seen Renoa run.

I FOUND HER AT THE NORTH END of the village where the forest begins. The fire had chased the wild animals to the edge of the forest where they prowled, caught between their fear of fire and their fear of man. There Renoa had run into them, with her apronful of wild animal dolls.

When I found her body, her face was gone and her legs and arms were chewed to the bone. I did not care if the animals ate me. I covered her body with dry leaves, her body with its face gone, its legs and arms chewed. I left her there for worms to devour and spiders to crawl upon. Then I walked to the nearest twist of the river. I laid my body in the icy-cold river and watched as the fire roared over the village, devouring it, and the sky black and blue above.

So it was that our village was destroyed, the crops burned, the haystacks burned, and our flocks roasted. It was the act of Renoa throwing Annakey's valley doll into the fire that did it. They were both Dollmages, and for a purpose, but I did not see clearly why until now. I will explain, and I must hurry. Still the robber people haunt the outskirts of our village, becoming bolder now that we are bereft. They no longer wish only to eat our grain and steal our children. They wish to make sport of our lives. There is little time left.

How it broke my heart to see you, my people, gathered on the bank of the river, talking in low tones to your children. I walked among you, counting you, and you looked at me with vacant eyes.

"What shall become of us, Dollmage?" you asked me. I did not have the heart to remind you that I was wise, not all-knowing.

"Look, up on Mount Crownantler. You see how the mountain has been untouched by the fire? There are sheep in that summer meadow," I said.

I left you there on the riverbank, almost knowing what you were plotting in your fear and devastation.

I found Annakey picking among the ruins of my house. She had unearthed some of the Sacred dolls, and some of the scorched and shriveled village doll of Seekvalley. She was running her hand over it.

"Make a new one, Dollmage," she said as I approached.

After a time she raised her head to look at me.

"You are the Dollmage now, Annakey," I said. "You must be. Renoa is dead."

Annakey put her hand over her eyes, then drew it away and stood.

"But how? I have broken my promise to marry Areth. For a villager, there is a way, for a Dollmage none."

"Lead me to the place where you have hidden the valley doll you made. Quickly, before the villagers gather themselves against you, before they are done their mourning."

She held my hand and led me across the valley to her secret place. The fire had not cut its path there, but the smoke hung like a fog over the river and ash fell like snow.

The valley doll she had made was in ashes in the fire Renoa had built.

"You have been making the story of the village for some time now, Annakey," I said.

"I had to do it, for my father."

"And for yourself?" As long as I must speak the truth, let it all be said. She did not deny. "Now you will begin again, and you will make a valley doll that will tell the end, the proper end. Begin."

On her flat rock, Annakey began once again to fashion it. I helped her, teaching her, encouraging her, pouring out all my knowledge at once. She knew so much intuitively, she had learned so much by watching me. She worked furiously until dark fell, hurried on by the fire. She stood back from her work.

She was horrified.

It was not Seekvalley village at all. It was wrong somehow. The mountains not as high, the river not as twisty, the rolling hills not so rolly.

"I cannot replicate our valley," she said.

I knew myself what it meant.

Annakey had not remade this valley for us. It was too late for this valley. We had to move to a new valley, and with her art, Annakey had found it. It was the very valley I had halfheartedly made for Fedr Rainsayer to find, but mine had been without true art, without belief. This was the valley that would be found, and there was the deer-trod and the nettle, the owl and the wild corn. By her art, we would see it and know it. The sheep in the summer meadow would not feed us until the valley was grown again. They would be left behind to distract the robber people while we escaped.

I wept for my valley. "You sorrow for my poor work," Annakey said.

"No," I answered. "It is good. Now make an ending for yourself. Then we must face the villagers and plead for your life."

She worked a little longer. In the dim light, I could not see what she did. When she was done she took my hand, and led me, blind in the dark, back to the village.

WHILE WE WERE GONE, you built little fires on the banks to warm yourselves. You made rude comments about your fires, insulting them, making yourselves feel bigger than the fire that had destroyed everything you had. That night you feasted on roast sheep and pig and chicken, and as you ate Areth talked loudly, telling his own story, and none of it true. You talked and talked, and the more you talked, the more you blamed Annakey. I hid her, knowing if you found her, she would be executed. "I will pray," I said to her, "then I will return for you." I walked to the place where the village doll lay charred. Among the ruins I found my husband's ghost doll. I brushed him off and put him in my pocket. Then I went to seek him at the forest's edge where Renoa's bones lay scattered like blown and broken branches. I stooped there a moment to pray. That was when the stranger appeared to me in the darkness. I thought he was a wild man, a man of the robber people.

"Dollmage Hobblefoot," he said in our own tongue. The robber people do not speak our language.

"I am she," I said. What was it about the man? Had I seen him before? I peered beneath the beard and long hair that hid his face.

"What has happened to the village?" he asked. "The ashes are still warm. The robber people . . . ?"

I nodded.

"Did all survive?"

"Only Renoa, Mabe's daughter, died. Oda Weedbridge is taken by the robber people. Annakey's life is yet in danger." I spoke as if to a ghost.

"I know nothing of Annakey or Renoa. What of Vilsa?"

Then I knew him, and you know him, too.

This is my secret. It was Annakey's father, returned. Not dead. I told him about Vilsa's faith and love, and about the daughter he did not know. With him I returned to where I had secreted Annakey. She was gone, and I found her bound and beaten, and all of you drunk with desire to stone her.

Now I say, Fedr Rainsayer, come forth!

Ah, Annakey, now you weep. Death by stoning could not make you weep, but this, yes. And how all of you look away, ashamed. A fine greeting it is for Fedr to come home and find his wife dead and his daughter bound by ropes. But I have begged his patience, and he has become a patient man in his travels.

Tell me if I do not speak the truth, Fedr, when I say that the mountains blinded you and your companion as you traveled. You suffered much from hunger and thirst and cold. You could find no passes. You came to great mountains, and sheltered yourselves in caves. You lost track of days and years. In spring you would remember your loved ones, and the promise you had made, and you would move on.

At last you found a valley. It was a beautiful valley. It was so much like Seekvalley that your companion, who died on the journey back, thought you had traveled in a circle and come home. You showed him how the mountains were not so high, the river not so twisty, and the rolling hills not so rolly. You named it Promise Valley, for those who died fulfilling the promise they made to find new land for your people. The soil is good for corn and melons, and there is plenty of water.

In fact, Fedr Rainsayer, it is just like the valley Annakey made.

I see now that there should indeed have been two Dollmages: one, Renoa, to lead some of the people to the new valley; the other, Annakey, to be Dollmage in Seekvalley. Renoa was meant to run wild, to know the secrets of mountains and trees and rivers and winds.

I see your hearts have changed as you murmur among yourselves. You no longer desire to stone Annakey, but for one.

You, Areth, will you not put down your stone? Will you not? No, Areth, do not strike her, your Dollmage, the one who will lead you to a new valley. Areth! Areth . . .

So then.

And now.

It is not only Manal that you had to be wary of, Areth, but Fedr also, and now he has killed you. Did you forget that he, too, was entitled to one stone? Fedr has become a wild man, wandering for years among the wild mountains. Even still, your ghost grasps at stones, Areth. Grasp at stones, then, past the time you have forgotten why.

Fedr, hold your daughter, as you dreamed of holding your

wife again. Now, Fedr, embrace your son-in-law, Manal, for I will wed them. It will be my last act as Dollmage.

Greppa, put down your stone. The bloodletting is done. A death will atone for the broken promise indeed, but it will not be Annakey's death. It will be mine. I will not go with you to the new valley that has been found, to the long lakes in the valley. Annakey will go as your Dollmage, and I will stay here among the ashes.

Mine is the death that will atone for Annakey's broken promise.

[Chapter 13]

INSCRIPTION ON THE SEEKVALLEY DOLL:
Seek by lake, by river and pond,
For this is the art of beyond.

GO NOW. MY TALE IS ENDED.

Or rather, Annakey's tale. Now you know how I could tell all the stories from her eyes. She is the Dollmage. She has been for some time. It is a wonder I have lived until now. Some few of you will miss me.

Do not weep so much. When I was young, I was a lace veil, pretty, but easy to see through. As I became a woman of mature years, I was a brown field, not beautiful but fruitful and fine. Now I am an old plough, toothless and tending to creak in the joints, but having done my share of the work. Leave me in the meadow and let the flowers grow up around me and I will be beautiful again. Besides, my husband is here to make me laugh and keep me company, and we will be with Renoa, whose spirit runs wild in the forest.

Do not be afraid of your gift, Annakey. Those who love you will only love you more for it, and you will free others to glory in their own goodness and beauty. You have already taught them that the most important promise is the one made to oneself. You have begun to teach them the ways to be happy.

You, Bontha Hogweigher, you will do well to follow her

example as your new Dollmage. You smile at me to scorn me. What is there to glory about me? you say. I walk like a goose and I sing like a horse. Worst of all, you say, I am bossy to all those who will let me boss them. What is good and loving and powerful in me?

I will tell you, Bontha, and we will see if any will deny. You, Bontha, make the best bread in the valley. You make the best buns and pies, too. Many a single man there is in the valley who has sat at night thinking it might be worth letting you boss him, if only he might eat your bread and pastry every day. But when the other women praise your bread, you shush them and mock their praise and refuse to accept your glory. Why? Because you are afraid.

Only pride is to be feared, only enmity with God and man.

You do not understand my stories? What does it matter? Annakey is the Dollmage now. Leave me. Follow Fedr Rainsayer to your new valley. It is beautiful, for I have seen it through the vision of Annakey's hands.

Go, Annakey, and make your new valley a place where a promise is not something you break your heart upon, but a word that binds hearts. Make your valley a place where a promise is not an end, but a beginning. Make your valley a place where words are not an enemy to truth and reason, and where the promise is a mother that nurtures, a lover that calls, not a weapon that bruises.

Keep your memory dolls and remember me always as one who loved you, my people. Honor your new Dollmage. Remember I told you the truth so that the words and the real might be one again, giving you power. Remember me, and love me anyway.

About the Author

Martine Leavitt is the award-winning author of the Marmawell Trilogy, which includes *The Dragon's Tapestry, The Prism Moon* and *The Taker's Key,* all published under the name Martine Bates. She is the mother of seven children, four of whom are grown.She lives in High River, Alberta, with her husband and her three younger children, and is presently pursuing a Master of Fine Arts degree at Vermont College.